END OF DAYS

AN ARKANE THRILLER
J.F. PENN

End of Days. An ARKANE Thriller Book 9
Copyright © J.F.Penn (2017). All rights reserved.

www.JFPenn.com

ISBN: 978-1-912105-65-6

Requests to publish work from this book should be sent to:
joanna@CurlUpPress.com

Cover and Interior Design: JD Smith Design

Printed by Lightning Source

www.CurlUpPress.com

For Jonathan.

Thank you for being by my side in Israel.

"Then I saw an angel coming down from heaven, holding in his hand the key to the bottomless pit and a great chain. And he seized the dragon, that ancient serpent, who is the devil and Satan, and bound him for a thousand years, and threw him into the pit, and shut it and sealed it over him … until the thousand years were ended."

Revelation 20:1-6

"The female of Samael is called Serpent, Woman of Harlotry, End of All Flesh, End of Days."

The demon Lilith, as described by Rashi, a medieval commentator on the Talmud and the Hebrew Scriptures

PROLOGUE

Two weeks ago. Ruins of Babylon, Iraq.

IT WAS DARK WHEN Massoud went back to the tomb. The moon was high and silver light glinted on the sands of Babylon, like the edge of a knife before it lodged in the heart of its prey. The sound of the camp filtered across the dunes, the crackling of fire and the voices of men trying to forget what they had seen in the light of day. Their tales of bravado steeled them to face another dawn.

But Massoud could not forget.

He clutched his tool bag tighter and scrambled across the ruins towards the edge of the excavations. Before the war, Saddam Hussein had been rebuilding the ancient city and much had been renewed. The tyrant had remounted the Lion of Babylon, a black rock sculpture over 2600 years old, and carved his own name into bricks alongside that of the ancient king, Nebuchadnezzar. For the glory of Iraq, he had said.

But now Saddam was dead and gone. Iraq was broken by war and crushed under the feet of fundamentalists, fighting for the scraps of what remained. This ancient city had been pounded by mortar and bulldozed by western soldiers, grinding what was left of proud Babylon into the dust of the desert. Massoud shook his head. It was all madness, but for now at least, there was good money to be made digging for archaeologists who wanted to make their names in the desert once more.

And there was a way to make more than just the daily cash in hand.

It was dangerous but it was worth the risk. There were those who would pay handsomely for a piece of ancient Babylon if it could be smuggled out, and he had glimpsed something earlier today at the very edge of his patch. If he could just get it out then his family would not go hungry this winter and his daughter would have her medicine.

A sound came from up ahead. A scuff of boots on stone and the hacking cough of a night watchman.

Massoud froze and ducked down behind a rock. If he was found here at this time of night, he could be beaten ... or worse. His heart pounded and his tongue stuck to the roof of his dry mouth.

But then the clouds shifted over the moon and darkness hid him as the guard passed only meters away. Massoud scurried to the tomb, clambering over the remains of the military base. He reached the very edge of the dig where they excavated part of the city that had not been explored before, revealing treasures unseen for millennia, a glimpse of its great past. Babylon had once been the largest city in the world, a hub of commerce and art and the pinnacle of civilization. Massoud smiled and shook his head. How the mighty had fallen indeed. A lesson that the Americans would learn some day, as the British and every other empire learned before them. Man was not built to last and days of glory passed quickly in the blink of history. All that mattered were the people you loved in this lifetime, and that was why he was here now.

He made it to the tomb and crouched at the edge of the pit that led to the entrance. His fingers dug into the red dirt and he hesitated as he felt a shadow at his back. He turned his head quickly.

There was no one there.

He shivered, then took a deep breath, steeling himself before clambering down into the pit. He pushed aside the wooden barrier and crawled within. He couldn't risk the torch yet, not this close to the entrance so he scrabbled in the dark, feeling his way.

Massoud breathed in the air of the tomb. He had dug at many ruins in the deserts of Iraq and he knew the smell of a ruined city. This one was not like the others. Where before he had smelled only the dust of the long dead, here he could smell the earth, freshly turned, as if something was alive down here.

As if the city could spring awake again.

He crawled into the darkness and felt the shadow of a presence, slipping along behind him in the dirt. A whisper in the dark.

The crackle of dry skin rasping across sand.

Sweat broke out on his brow but he kept going. He couldn't turn his head in the narrow tunnel and he knew he would see nothing anyway. Perhaps it was a djinn of the desert, a demon of this cursed city. But there were so many demons in Iraq now and Massoud was more afraid of the human kind than the ethereal. The extremists had taken his cousin away one night and his body had never been found. They had beaten his old father in the market when all he had done was play music at his stall. Yes, the demons in human form that stalked the country now were surely worse than anything under the sands. Massoud crawled on.

At last he made it to the dogleg in the tunnel, out of direct sight of the entrance. He turned on his head-torch. The dull yellow light drove away the shadows and finally he crawled into the tomb itself. Lamplight flickered across rough-hewn walls, revealing a mosaic in bright colors, undimmed by buried years. It was both magnificent and terrible, the image searing itself on his memory. A massive serpent undulated across a map of the known world, its mouth gaping to swallow a bound woman. Its hooked fangs pierced the body of a screaming sacrifice while its huge coils wrapped around countless other dead. Massoud couldn't read the cuneiform text below the serpent, but he had been in enough tombs to know that it was a warning.

When the archaeologists had opened the tomb a few days ago, they had found myriad skeletons of long-dead snakes amongst human bones, evidence of sacrifice to this demon serpent. Massoud shivered to think of being left down here in the dark with hissing death. A primeval terror, especially for a desert people.

Suddenly, he heard a slither in the dark. Something moved at the edge of the torchlight, just outside the warm glow.

Massoud jerked his head around.

Were there still snakes down here?

Stop being a fool, he chastised himself. *The faster this is done, the faster you can get out of here and turn this old stone into a fortune.*

He turned back to the wall. A black stone slab lay at the corner of the mosaic, carved with the giant serpent on a smaller scale against an inlaid pattern of stars. Cuneiform text wound around it, disappearing into the rock beyond. He couldn't excise the whole slab, but it was still a priceless piece of art that was also small enough for him to smuggle out.

He pulled his mason's hammer and chisel from his tool belt and bent to place the blade carefully behind the stone slab. The metallic tapping obscured the rustle of snake skin from behind him in the shadows. The sound echoed down into the depths of the earth, calling to the darkness to rise again.

CHAPTER 1

Appalachian Mountains, Kentucky, USA.

LILITH STEPPED OVER THE threshold into the tiny church. The white walls were duller than she remembered, marred by time and stained by the breath of believers, reeking of tobacco and the residue of communion wine. It had been years since she had visited, but the smell of the place instantly took her back to her childhood. Back then, the Appalachian Pentecostal church had been her home, her escape, the only place where she felt part of something bigger in a miserable life of poverty.

She had come a long way since then.

Lilith wore a shapeless dress of muted color, the traditional style for women in these parts, having left her smart tailored clothes behind in the city. Her face was bare of makeup and her titian curls hung loose about her shoulders. Her work colleagues at Viperex Pharmaceuticals wouldn't even recognize her.

But she needed this. She had been away too long. There was something only this place could give her and today, she was coming home.

Orphaned as a toddler, Lilith had passed from foster family to foster family around the poor neighborhoods on the border of Kentucky and Virginia. She had a propensity for silence and shied away when people tried to hug her.

These things kept her apart and made even the most loving mothers think she was touched in some way. Then one day, here in this church, she had discovered that which brought her alive. She had never been drawn to people, but here she had found her true passion.

In the last month, the serpents had called her back, haunting her sleep. She woke most nights with her hands in the air, reaching for the weight of them, wanting to dance. Perhaps today …

"Hello dear." Lilith jumped as a woman touched her arm. "Are you visiting with us today?"

Lilith turned and looked down at her. There was something familiar in the hunched frame, the faint smell of lavender and the woman's pattern of missing teeth.

"Are you sister Beatrice?" Lilith narrowed her eyes a little, trying to remember.

"Why, yes, child. I am. How would you know?" The woman looked more closely at her. Then a smile lit up her face, making her blue eyes crinkle and the gaps in her teeth protrude even more. "You're Lily. Well my goodness, it's been many years since we've seen you here, sweetie. Since that day …" Her words trailed off as her eyes dimmed at the memory. Then she patted Lilith on the arm. "Well now, you're welcome back. I'm sure Pastor John will be pleased to see you."

The woman bustled away as the small community filled the church and the sound of greetings filled the air. Lilith stood at the back in a white wooden pew, eyes down and demure. She clutched a hymn sheet in shaking hands, anticipating the service to come. She didn't want to draw attention to herself – not yet, anyway.

The plinky-plonk of piano keys filled the room and the congregation stood to sing a rousing folk song with clapping and shouts of praise interspersing the notes. Some shook tambourines, the rattle of tin beating time. The energy in the room stepped up a notch and Lilith felt the rise of a smile on her lips, buoyed by the faithful who came here to escape their miserable lives every Sunday.

"I'm going to tell you children, do you know what Jesus Christ said?" Pastor John began in his singsong voice, the final words rising to a high note. He stepped forward, his hands raised towards heaven.

And at his feet, a locked box.

Lilith couldn't stop looking at it. She knew what was in there even though she couldn't hear the rattle from this far away. Her eyes stayed fixed on it as Pastor John continued, his tone rising and falling as his flock thrust their hands high.

"And the gospel of Saint Mark says that these signs shall follow them that believe. IN MY NAME they will cast out devils, and speak with new tongues. IN MY NAME they shall take up serpents and if they drink any deadly thing, it shall not hurt them. IN MY NAME, they shall lay hands on the sick and they shall recover."

"Hallelujah!"

"Praise Jesus!"

A man a few meters in front of Lilith began to shake in place, his whole body wracked with convulsions. Those around him calmly laid hands upon him and prayed. Another woman fell to her knees in the aisle, crying and speaking in tongues.

Lilith watched, waiting for the atmosphere to rise even further, for the spirit-fueled hysteria to grow. Back in her university days, when she had trained as a scientist, she had researched mass hysteria and tried to explain away what happened in this little corner of the world. Some would say these people were caught up in the Spirit, others would think they were crazy. Lilith was still unsure what she believed, but her own truth lay inside that locked box.

As the piano thumped into another tune, Pastor John bent and opened the lid.

"When God anoints you, when the Spirit prompts you, you can take up serpents IN HIS NAME!"

Lilith's heart raced as she caught a glimpse of the snakes within. Three timber rattlesnakes, deep brown chevron markings on their muscled bodies. She ached to touch them, to feel their cool skin against hers. She licked her lips, hardly able to stay in place.

Pastor John lifted out one of the snakes and held it high. It wrapped itself around his wrist, tongue flickering as it tasted the air. He bounced to the music, shuffling around and singing loud as it wound around his hands.

The man who had been convulsing just a few minutes ago stepped into the aisle. His forehead gleamed with sweat and patches of it formed under his armpits, staining his shirt. He fixed his eyes on the snake as songs of praise swelled and filled the little church.

Those who spoke in tongues shouted their guttural praise to the Lord as the man walked to the front of the church.

Pastor John nodded at him and held out the rattlesnake. From behind, Lilith could see cords of muscle on his back standing out through his sweat-drenched shirt. His fear was palpable and she knew the snakes would sense it.

He reached out for the rattlesnake.

Lilith clutched the edge of the pew, her heart hammering at what could happen if the rattler struck him. But the snake seemed merely bemused by its handling, curious to taste the skin of the man. Its flickering tongue tasted his salt, head wavering over his arm.

She relaxed a little at the snake's behavior, confident that it wouldn't bite him for now. Lilith was a herpetologist by day, working with snakes in a lab where they were specimens to be tested, farmed and milked to make anti-venom. She understood snakes' body language but in the lab, she was a scientist, clinically detached.

Whereas here the serpents were primal beings, and she craved their touch.

More in the congregation were shaking and crying now, the frenzy growing. The pianist just kept playing as people stamped and prayed, some falling down.

"Getting high on Jesus is better than cocaine," a man next to Lilith said with a toothy grin, as he joined the growing number of dancers in the aisle.

A woman brought her baby up to Pastor John. With one hand he cradled the child and with the other, he picked up another rattlesnake from the box.

"IN MY NAME they shall take up serpents and if they drink any deadly thing, it shall not hurt them. And we claim this now for your child, Lord."

Lilith felt an echo of her once-strong faith. She had been the youngest child in the congregation to handle snakes at aged seven, considered a blessing on the church, a miracle of sorts. Until that day …

It was time to face them again.

She stepped into the aisle, her green eyes fixed on Pastor John, who held the baby in the crook of one arm, the snake in his other hand.

He looked up and saw her approach. His eyes narrowed and then recognition sparked.

"Praise Jesus," he called aloud. "A daughter returned."

But Lilith could see hesitation in his eyes. He remembered. She had taken up serpents nearly every week until her fifteenth year, when she had been struck.

Pastor John had handed her the snake that day.

She remembered the initial sting, the shock of the hit, and then burning physical pain as the venom had raced through her blood. Her arm had begun to swell immediately and the world had swayed and then collapsed into colors and sounds.

Lilith remembered a curious jealousy in the eyes of those who had watched her fall to the ground. She had been given a chance to test her faith. Would the Lord take her? Was it her time? Or would she demonstrate faith by not succumbing to the poison?

They had laid her in the Pastor's office on a blanket and prayed for her and over her and with her. Whispered words of faith in the hallucinations of the night, but nothing for the pain.

No hospital treatment. No anti-venom.

Just the rustle of snake skin in the dark.

Then she had recovered just as the Lord had promised. A sign to the faithful. But fear had crept in and she had never handled in church again. She had stolen money and run to the city. Over time, she had been drawn back to snakes, training as a herpetologist and working for one of the foremost producers of anti-venom.

Now years later, she was back here again.

Lilith held out her hands, her eyes fixed on Pastor John.

"I take up serpents because the Bible says I will not be harmed," she said calmly, loud enough for him to hear over the music. "It is the confirmed word of God."

She knew he couldn't deny her the chance. He nodded and handed her the rattler.

Lilith took hold of it. The heaviness of its body, the smooth scales, so cool to her touch. She raised it to her face, let its tongue flicker over her features, let it taste her. It felt like coming home and she wanted more.

She bent and picked the final snake from the box, letting it wrap around her other arm. Then she reached out to the sweating man and lightly took the rattler from his shaking hands. The relief in his eyes was palpable and he fell to his knees in prayer.

Now Lilith had three rattlesnakes winding around her, two in one hand and one in the other. She raised her arms high, standing still and silent while the congregation whirled and stamped around her. Tambourines rattled. The faithful cried out to their God. She closed her eyes and felt the power of the serpent running through her, like a current into the ground beneath. Its ancient power rising and channeling through her blood.

Then she felt it. A whisper like that in her dreams.

The heartbeat of the Serpent of Serpents.

He was coming.

CHAPTER 2

London, England.

"MORGAN, JAKE. WAIT." THE deep voice boomed through the corridor of the ARKANE headquarters, deep under Trafalgar Square in central London.

Dr Morgan Sierra turned to see Director Marietti at the entrance to one of the labs. He held a cane and rested against the door frame. His body was still weak from the injuries he had sustained in India during the hunt for the Brahmastra weapon, but his eyes were steel hard. Morgan knew that he would not back down in the face of danger, whether inside ARKANE or out in the world. She was part of that fight now and even though they had just returned from a mission, she was ready for whatever came next.

Jake went to Marietti and embraced his mentor, then stepped back, aware that he might have overstepped the mark. But Marietti smiled.

"It's good to see you back safely." He looked at Morgan. "Both of you."

Marietti's eyes met hers. They had almost come to blows over her actions in India, when she had made a decision against his orders, but it seemed that was now forgotten. His words were as close to an apology as she was likely to get.

And that was OK.

"I know you've just returned," Marietti continued, "but

there's something we need to work on urgently. Something that may threaten us all."

He beckoned them into the lab. Morgan followed Jake into the room, one of the sterile environments used for examining ancient artifacts, down in the hidden chambers that few knew about. The public-facing side of the Arcane Religious Knowledge And Numinous Experience Institute consisted of funding academic discourse on religious topics, but ARKANE was actually a secret agency investigating supernatural mysteries around the world. There were secrets down in the vault below that Morgan had almost died to protect and many more left to uncover.

Like the artifact Marietti pointed at now.

Spotlights illuminated a black marble tablet mounted on its side. Even with the bright lights in the room, the temperature felt cooler around the slab, as if the stone sucked in the light and warmth around it.

Morgan shivered a little as she bent to look at the tablet more closely. It was roughly cut around the edges, as if excavated in a hurry and one end was missing. A huge serpent curled across the face of a map of the known earth as it was millennia ago. Its jaws gaped wide and its fangs dripped poison as it pierced the body of a sacrifice heaped upon a pile of corpses. People cowered around it, some rapt in worship, others with faces contorted by terror. The precise chisel marks of cuneiform text ran around the tableau.

"The cuneiform words tell of an ancient evil."

A man stepped from the shadows in the corner of the room. He wore a black amaranth-piped cassock with pellegrina, a purple fascia and a gold pectoral cross. A scarlet skullcap topped his white close-cropped hair. His eyebrows were bushy above piercing blue eyes and he moved with the silent, lithe grace of an athlete.

"This is Cardinal Eric Krotalia," Marietti said. "He's an expert on eschatology, the End Times. I've been consulting with him about the tablet. He's one of our ARKANE advocates in Rome."

"Good to meet you, sir." Jake held out his hand and Krotalia shook it firmly.

Morgan thought Marietti's tone was just a little reserved, but if he trusted the Cardinal then she should respect his opinion. She nodded a greeting but kept her distance at the other end of the table. The man was just a little too good looking for a Cardinal, more like Sean Connery playing the aged hero than a crusty Vatican scholar.

Cardinal Krotalia walked up to the table and pointed at the carving.

"According to legend, the serpent will appear at the End of Days to devour the earth. The language is close to some of the biblical prophecies, although of course this tablet is much older than extant texts."

Marietti's dark eyes were haunted at he gazed at the marble. "It was smuggled out of Iraq as part of a network of archaeologists trying to save what's left of ancient civilizations. After the destruction of Palmyra, there are many who worry what else may be lost in the darkness of religious extremism."

Morgan reached out a finger to touch the edge of the slab. It was exciting to be this close to a piece of that iconic civilization and one of the reasons she loved working for ARKANE. "The mythology of the snake is in every culture," she said. "Why is this tablet so important?"

"Because of the timing." Marietti pointed to one part of the marble slab. "This references a particular pattern of rarely seen star constellations. We've cross-referenced with data from multiple sources and this particular stellar alignment only occurs once every four thousand years. This one coincides with a series of blood moon eclipses that intersect with Serpens, part of the constellation Ophiuchus, believed to represent Laocoon –"

"– who was killed by sea serpents," Morgan finished for him.

"Let me guess," Jake said, raising an eyebrow. "It's happening soon."

As he spoke, Martin Klein entered the lab. ARKANE's brilliant archivist bobbed up and down on the balls of his feet and brushed his ragged blonde hair back from his face. He pushed his wire-rimmed spectacles further up the ridge of his nose as he spoke with excitement, his words tumbling over one another.

"You're right, Jake! The alignment will happen in only ten days and we will be here to witness it." Martin grinned and clapped his hands a little, bouncing in place like a child delighted with a new toy. "What was prophesied so many thousand years ago will now come to pass."

Marietti held his hand up and Martin stopped bouncing, his smile fading at the Director's grim face. "While this *is* academically exciting on the one hand, it's also worrying. The text tells of a serpent who will destroy the earth, a warning of apocalypse at a time when too many already seek oblivion for humankind."

The Cardinal raised his hands as he intoned the words from the book of Revelation. "He seized the dragon, that ancient serpent, who is the devil and Satan, and bound him for a thousand years, and threw him into the pit, and shut it and sealed it over him … until the thousand years were ended."

"But the serpent is a representation of many things," Morgan said, resisting the pronunciation of doom. "Renewal in the shedding of skin, rebirth and eternity in the ouroboros, the snake eating its own tail. Why are you so worried about this in particular?"

Marietti sat down heavily on a chair by the marble tablet. The penumbra of the spotlight caught the side of his craggy face, deepening the shadows under his eyes. His skin was sallow, his shoulders drooped. Morgan saw a broken man on the edge of what he could handle. Marietti sighed and shook his head.

"I haven't told you what's been going on at ARKANE these last few months. The hierarchy and politics are generally kept hidden from field agents, so you can concentrate on your jobs. But you know ARKANE has teams all over the world, across many faiths and cultural divides. Up until recently, we all agreed that the supernatural world we face should be kept away from the public."

He shook his head and the Cardinal continued for him.

"Now it seems there are some who want to hasten the End Times, those who believe the Great Battle should come soon, and who believe that in trying to keep the supernatural away from the world, ARKANE somehow blocks the cosmic plan. We are concerned that this serpent will be used somehow to hasten the End of Days. When Director Marietti told me of the tablet, I knew we had to act."

"Sounds just as crazy as what we usually face out there," Jake said. "So what can we do?"

"The cuneiform script tells of a great pit where the serpent lies bound," Marietti said. "An echo of the Revelation verse, so I give it some credence. I want you both to find the pit, because others search for it too."

Martin picked up his tablet computer, fingers flashing across the screen. "The group we suspect to be involved wears this symbol." He turned it round to show Morgan and Jake a tattoo of a coiled snake poised to strike, inked in emerald green. "They call themselves Roshites."

"From the Hebrew word *rosh*, meaning poison or venom," Morgan said, recalling the Hebrew. Although she hadn't lived in Israel for a number of years now, she had been brought up there by her father, murdered as one of the Remnant, and Hebrew was her second, fluent language. She felt a fleeting need to speak it again as the word formed on her lips. She thought differently when she spoke the ancient language, even dreamed different dreams.

"Indeed," Martin continued. "The Roshites are devotees of the Great Serpent, an ancient sect that can be tracked through history. The snake goddess sculptures at Knossos depict women holding writhing serpents aloft. Then there's the prophetess Pythia of the Delphic oracle in ancient Greece. Wadjet, the snake goddess of the uraeus crown in Egypt. And then of course, the biblical history –"

"The brazen serpent on Moses' staff," Morgan interrupted. "So that when anyone was bitten by a snake, they could look at the bronze idol and be healed. From the book of Numbers, chapter twenty-one."

Jake had been quiet but now he spoke. "And let's not forget this ancient serpent of Revelation, bound and cast into a pit, until the thousand years are ended. That seems to be the most important aspect right now."

Marietti put his hand on Jake's shoulder. "That's what I fear. It seems that the serpent was buried to keep it from the world, so at least our ancestors were able to vanquish it once before. But this prophecy suggests it is coming again."

"Perhaps it's just allegory," Morgan said. "The sin of the world, the knowledge of good and evil, that's what is destroying the earth. The Anthropocene era, as they call it now, demonstrates how man has brought this destruction upon himself."

Marietti looked at her, his eyes full of sorrow. "I wish it were so, Morgan. But you've seen the other side of allegory as an ARKANE agent. You know what we have to keep from those outside." He gestured down towards the vault beneath them. "You know the secrets we keep. You saw the demon in the bone church, the creatures from the Gates of Hell, the power of the Brahmastra. How can you now doubt that this could also be real?"

Morgan smiled. "You can't take the scientist out of the girl. But I take your point." She ran a finger over the curls of the snake, following its path across the slab. "This isn't uniform," she said. "Perhaps it's some kind of map?"

"My thoughts exactly." Martin tapped on the tablet again and spun it around. "This is a map of ancient Iraq and I've indicated the possible route of the snake based on the undulations on the slab. It heads directly east through Asia and out into the Western Pacific. Beyond the boundaries of what they would have known as the earth at the time, right out into the ocean."

"Whatever it was, it looks like they went to a lot of effort to get rid of it." Jake pinched the screen and zoomed in on the map. "That's near the Mariana Trench, the deepest place on earth."

"Not somewhere we can just rock up and search then," Morgan noted.

"There is something else." Marietti took the tablet from Martin and pulled up an image of the Ishtar Gate, a massive arch with bright blue bricks decorated with images of dragons and aurochs bulls. "The tablet was found at the back of where the Ishtar Gate was originally excavated. But there's information missing so perhaps there is a more detailed clue at the gate."

"Guess we're heading to Iraq then." Jake smiled. "It's been a while."

Actually, it's closer than that," Marietti said. "The Ishtar Gate is in Berlin at the Pergamon Museum."

"I'll make the arrangements." Martin tapped on his device. "By the time you've swapped your gear over from the India trip, you'll be good to go back out."

Morgan and Jake walked out into the corridor, heading for the weapons room. It was a short turnaround but they could kit up and be on their way again later tonight. Morgan loved the adrenalin of the mission and was keen to get going.

But there was one thing she had to know before they left. One thing that could put them both in grave danger.

CHAPTER 3

Appalachian Mountains, Kentucky, USA. 10:12pm.

LILITH'S EYES FLICKED OPEN, suddenly wide with the knowledge of what was coming. As she gasped with the rush, she saw a man at the back of the church. His dark eyes were fixed on her. His close-cropped hair receded over a broad forehead, green eyes so like her own staring back at her. He wore a black shirt open two buttons and she could see a tattoo winding up his neck. The coils of a serpent in green and yellow.

He beckoned to her, then turned and walked out of the church.

Lilith felt the serpents shift in her hands. She had lost control and they would soon grow restless. As the faithful continued to sing, she bent and placed the three snakes back into their box at the feet of Pastor John.

Then she ran from the church out into the night.

The man leaned against the bonnet of a weathered SUV, his features shrouded in darkness. He was tall and powerfully muscled, with the scuffed boots and latent power of a ranger in the mountains.

"I know you felt it," the man said, his voice sensual, languid. "Do you want to know more?"

Lilith took a step towards him.

"Know more about what?" Her voice sounded fragile out

here in the night, drowned out by the singing still audible in the church behind her.

The man went to the door of the car and opened it. The light from inside lit his face from beneath, his eyes dark hollows. He pulled his shirt away from his neck to reveal more of the snake tattoo. Lilith found herself walking towards him until she could see the detail of each scale. She stood so close she could feel the heat from his body and smell the musk from his skin. She wanted to lick his flesh with an outstretched tongue like the rattlers would.

"The time of the Great Serpent is close," he whispered. "Those of us who practice mithridatism know it."

Lilith inhaled sharply and stepped back. How did he know of her secret addiction? The practice involved injecting small amounts of venom regularly, in order to build up immunity to the poison.

That's how it started anyway.

Deep down, Lilith knew she chased the high she felt in the depths of poisoning, the hallucinations that took her out of her body into another realm. The small amounts she self-administered took the edge off the craving, but she always wanted more. The toxins were building up in her blood – they could kill her at any time.

But she couldn't stop.

"There's a venom you haven't tried," the man whispered. "One that will take you into the realms of what I know you crave." He bent close to her ear. His breath made her shiver. "Because I crave it too."

Lilith's heart hammered in her chest. He was hypnotic, dominant. She wanted what he offered, in so many ways.

"Who are you?"

"My chosen name is Samael." He smiled, and Lilith heard a dark humor under his intensity. "Call me Sam. And you, Lilith …" He stepped closer to her, cupping her chin and lifting her face. "You were born to be part of this."

His lips brushed hers with the gentlest of touches and something in her blood called to him. But the coils of the Great Serpent lay heavy in her mind.

"Part of what?" she said, putting her hand on his chest and pushing him back.

Sam stepped away and reached into the car. He pulled out a tablet computer and swiped the screen a few times. He brought up a picture of the night sky and zoomed into a star system.

"This is Serpens, part of the constellation of Ophiuchus. The picture was taken two nights ago." He was all business now, speaking with authority as he swiped the screen again to display an image of a black marble tablet inlaid with the coils of a great snake. "This is a tablet from ancient Babylon, a prophecy that tells of the rising of the Great Serpent at the End Times." His eyes flashed with sudden anger. "That piece is lost to me now, but we have detailed photos. The pattern of the stars on the tablet match the constellation for the first time in four thousand years. My men are heading to Berlin to get the final piece of the puzzle, so we will soon know where the Great Serpent lies."

It sounded crazy and one part of Lilith, the scientist, wanted to mock his words. She would expect talk of the End Times and the Great Serpent from the fanatics inside the church. And yet, his words captivated her. Venom ran through her veins and his words made her blood sing.

"And then what?" she asked.

"Then we bring him back," Sam said, his eyes flashing with fire. "You felt the power of those tiny snakes here, so imagine how powerful the Serpent of Serpents will be. We will serve him and reign in a new world order. But I need your help."

The thought of this powerful man needing her brought a smile to Lilith's lips.

"Why? What can I do that you can't?"

Sam sighed and shook his head. Lilith sensed a form of jealousy running beneath. "There is no other who can handle the venom levels you have already survived. Believe me, we've tried a number of subjects and there's no time to waste anymore." Lilith fleetingly wondered who those subjects had been, and whether they had died in the spasms of venom poisoning.

"I've even tried myself, but you … you're the only one who can reach him." Sam's voice was flattering, even respectful as he continued. "I know you must have heard him in your dreams and in your venom trance. Only you can find him now. Come with me, please. Help me bring him back."

Sam reached into the car and pulled out a vacuum flask. He unscrewed the lid and a plume of dry ice wafted into the air with a puff of exhalation. He pulled out a tiny vial.

"If you come with me, this is yours."

Lilith reached out a hand for it, but Sam held it out of her reach.

"What is it?"

"Inland taipan."

Lilith gasped and the hairs on the back of her neck prickled, her skin rising in goosebumps. The inland taipan had the most toxic venom of any land snake in the world, ten times as venomous as the Mojave rattlesnake. The venom was also a legendary hallucinogen, incredibly dangerous but also rumored to give the user an experience out of time.

"You'll see the other side, Lilith. You'll experience pleasure unlike any you have before. Just come with me tonight and learn more. If you choose to leave later, then of course you can go back to your old life."

Sam put the vial back into the vacuum flask and sealed the top again. He walked around to the passenger side of the car and opened the door for her.

Lilith saw a new future in his eyes. One she wanted to be a part of. She had spent too long in the labs, clinically milking the snakes, reducing them to chemistry. She was easily replaceable by any other lab technician. But Samael offered a chance to be part of something greater. She had glimpsed the Great Serpent, and now she would tear down the veil to reach him.

And she wanted that venom.

Lilith got into the car.

They headed south until they reached a private airfield. A helicopter sat waiting, the pilot ready for takeoff.

"I'll bring you back if you change your mind," Sam said.

She walked towards the chopper. "I'm ready."

* * *

Grand Canyon Snake Valley Retreat, USA

Two hours later, they landed at a private helipad and Sam helped Lilith from the helicopter onto a path that led towards a lodge. The wind blew her hair about her face as they walked up the path. Artful spotlights in cactus beds lit the lodge in a subtle manner, giving the wood and stone a mottled effect that made it almost blend into the rocky ground.

"The Colorado river winds like a snake through the very earth of the United States," Sam said, as he led her into the lodge. It was stark inside, the walls decorated with a few chosen pieces. An Aboriginal dot painting of the Creation Snake. An enlarged photo of the head of a green mamba, the brilliant color bright against the white wall.

"Come outside." Sam beckoned and Lilith followed him out to a wide wooden deck that stretched out over the edge of the Grand Canyon.

The breeze wafted the night air over them, bringing the scent of sagebrush and ocotillo, the heady aromas of the mesa. Lilith stepped closer to the edge and looked down into the darkness below. The black deepened as the valley fell away before her and Lilith held the edge of the railing to steady herself as her vision adjusted. It was a long way down.

Sam came and stood behind her, his breath tickling her neck. Lilith wanted him to touch her, craved his lips on hers, but there was a question in her mind.

"How did you find me?" she asked softly.

"Viperex is my company," Sam said. "I heard the call of the Great Serpent when I was deep undercover in Africa years ago. I was drugged and scared, tied up in a cell, under threat of execution by terrorists. But the King of Snakes calmed me and when I made it out of there, I returned to the US and started Viperex."

He put his arms around her and she could feel his arousal against her back.

"The company attracts those who feel drawn to the serpent, and I let vials of venom be released for the mithridatists. I wanted to find those who could take it. Those who could take all of it."

He brushed her hair away from her neck and kissed her softly.

Then he bit down and she shivered at the sensation of his sharp teeth on her bare skin. He lifted his head and turned her to face him, his eyes dark with longing.

"I've been watching you for so long, Lilith. When the Babylon tablet was uncovered, I knew it was time."

Her name was soothing on his lips and as he bent to her, she closed her eyes, giving herself to the serpent within.

CHAPTER 4

London, England.

ONCE THEY WERE OUT of range of the lab, Morgan put a hand out and stopped Jake in the corridor. "Are you sure you're OK with this mission?" she asked, acutely aware that not so long ago, Jake had been bitten by a nest of vipers in the hunt for the Gates of Hell. The poison had left him on the edge of death and she knew it had broken something in his mind too, a phobia of snakes re-awakened from his childhood in South Africa.

Jake looked down at her, the corkscrew scar above his left eye crinkling a little as he smiled. His brown eyes were warm and inviting, like the first chestnuts of autumn. Morgan trusted him implicitly, but she couldn't let his phobia jeopardize the mission or their lives.

"Something happened when I was in New York," he said quietly. "I haven't told you, or anyone, the details." He shook his head in disbelief. "To be honest, I'm not sure how much of it was real. But you know I came back changed, you saw evidence of that in India. My body has healed and my mind too. I can't explain it, but –"

Morgan put a finger up to his lips, stopping his words. "If you're sure you can handle the whole snake thing, then I'm happy." She moved her hand to his chest, acutely aware of how close he was. She could feel the beat of his heart, slow and steady, and smell his pine forest aftershave. "Most of what I've seen with ARKANE has been inexplicable anyway," she continued. "If we ever have time to stop and think too much about it all, we'll both go nuts."

Jake smiled and put his hand over hers. "Maybe we can go nuts together."

A noise came behind them in the corridor. They broke apart quickly and walked away to get their gear for the mission.

* * *

Berlin, Germany.

Morgan shivered as they walked the back streets of Berlin towards the Pergamon Museum. The night air was cool and a light rain fell. She pulled her leather jacket closer about her as the sound of laughter drifted out of an all-night bar as they walked by.

"Fancy a drink?" Jake said, his voice low.

"Absolutely." Morgan smiled, wishing that they could just forget everything for a night. Jake raised an eyebrow and she gave a rueful smile. The apocalypse waited for no one. "But I guess we'll have to leave it for another time."

The city was young, a party town full of start-ups and trendy bars, but affordable enough that the tech and art scenes still thrived. Like London and Paris, Berlin never slept. But at this time of night, it was at least quieter, and they remained in the shadows as they headed towards Museum Island on the River Spree.

Morgan and Jake were no strangers to breaking and entering, but Martin had assured them that one of the local ARKANE agents would meet them at the museum and take them to the Ishtar Gate. They crossed a pedestrian bridge, turning away from the grand main entrance to walk down the side to a goods delivery door. A figure stood in the dark, the glow of a cigarette by his side. He raised a hand in greeting as they approached.

"I'm Christoph," he said, shaking their hands. "Berlin office."

He was young, Morgan noticed with a rueful smile, even though his hipster beard made him look older. His eyes weren't yet lined by the years and there was no evidence of pain in his body as he moved to open the door for them. She felt the scar from the demon's claw throb at her side and, for a moment, the exhaustion of India threatened to overcome her. The darkness made her want to sink down and sleep in a corner of this quiet place.

They walked into the museum along a service corridor, their footsteps echoing in the dim hallway.

"So, you're here to see the Ishtar Gate?" Christoph asked.

"We don't know what we're looking for exactly," Jake said. "But we have a stone tablet from Babylon that dates to the same period so we're looking for cuneiform inscriptions that might match."

Christoph stopped at a doorway. "This way." He grinned and Morgan couldn't help but smile at his infectious enthusiasm. "Brace yourself."

He pushed open the door and they stepped into a gigantic open space with high ceilings. In front of them stood a massive three-sided edifice, a reconstruction of the ancient Greek Pergamon Altar from the second century BC. Spotlights from below touched the faces of Olympian gods battling giants on a sculpture frieze. It was a piece of classical history brought to a modern world, a juxtaposition of the past in a city that surfed the web into the future.

"Pretty cool place to work, huh." Christoph led them to the right of the altar into another chamber dominated by a two-story marble structure. It loomed over them in the semi-darkness and Morgan was just able to make out ornate friezes covered in bulls and flowers.

"This is the Market Gate of Miletus," Christoph said. "We go through it to the Ishtar Gate. Come." He beckoned them to follow him through the middle arch.

As they stepped through, Morgan thought she heard something clang further out in the museum. It was faint and neither Christoph nor Jake seemed to hear it. But she still checked her gun in its shoulder holster. After some difficult moments in India, she wasn't going on a mission without a weapon for a while.

She stopped and listened for a moment but all was quiet again.

Christoph turned on more lighting in the room ahead.

"Wow!" Jake was clearly impressed and Morgan hurried to catch them. She emerged into another room, through the middle of the Ishtar Gate. After the dark night and the cool white marble of the ancient Greek monuments, the stunning colors of the edifice filled her vision.

The glazed bricks were cobalt blue, the color seemingly unfaded by time. It was decorated with bas-relief dragons and aurochs bulls in gold, symbolizing the gods Marduk and Adad. A flower frieze ran around the base, each petal perfectly rendered.

"It was constructed around 575 BC by King Nebuchadnezzar, the eighth gate to the inner city of Babylon," Christoph explained. "These are mostly the original bricks."

Morgan stepped closer to it, running her fingers lightly over one of the dragons. To think that Nebuchadnezzar himself had seen these bricks. She shook her head. It was truly amazing.

"You wanted cuneiform. Well, there is something strange on the side. An inscription that has puzzled Near Eastern scholars." Christoph led them around the side of the gate and pointed at a cuneiform inscription above a pattern of dots.

"The dots could be constellations?" Jake bent closer.

"Yes, they thought of that," Christoph said, "but there were no star patterns like this in ancient times."

"But did they check for when the stars might be in this alignment?" Morgan asked.

Christoph frowned. "I'm not sure, I'll have to find out. But there's something else. Down here."

As he bent to the lower bricks, a sound of movement came from the room beyond. Then a short exclamation of pain as someone tripped, wrong-footed in the dark.

Morgan and Jake pulled their weapons out.

Christoph froze. "I don't know who else could be here," he whispered. "But I'm sure it's fine, just one of the curators."

Morgan glanced quickly around. They were tucked into a corner out of the main line of sight, but if anyone walked through the gate, they would be seen. Perhaps it was just a night watchman, but something made her uneasy.

"I'll deal with it," Christoph said. Before they could stop him, he walked back out into the main hall. He pulled a notebook from his jacket and began to write something, looking up as if in surprise at the noise from beyond the gate.

"Hello," he said. "I'm just catching up on some research before the tourist horde arrives later. I wasn't expecting anyone else to be here."

He walked out of sight between the main pillars.

Round the corner, Jake nudged Morgan. "We've got to get out of here," he whispered, gesturing towards the darkness of the halls beyond, where they could just make out looming statues of Assyrian gods. "That way."

Morgan pulled out her smart phone and took a few silent pictures of the top inscription and the bricks that Christoph was about to explain. There was no time to figure out what they might mean and no way of getting the bricks out of the gate.

Then she peered round the corner.

Christoph backed into the main hall, his hands held up as if in surrender. He spoke in rapid German. Morgan knew enough to understand he was offering to help with anything they needed.

A man came into view, black hair pulled back into a ponytail and one side of his face drooping and disfigured as if he'd had a stroke. A tattoo of a serpent wound up and around his neck. He held a Glock in front of him, the gun pointing at Christoph's face. Two more men walked out behind him, one of them holding a large bag.

Morgan ducked back out of sight, gesturing for Jake to get down low. They could take the three men out between the two of them, but a firefight in central Berlin and bodies piled up in this eminent museum wasn't quite what she'd planned for tonight.

Plus it would hold them up, and she really needed that drink.

The voices faded a little and Morgan guessed that Christoph was leading the men round to the other side of the gate to look at an alternative inscription. She stuck her head out slowly. Sure enough, they were out of sight.

She indicated to Jake to stay low. They ran quickly and silently around the back edge of the hall, ducking down behind a table with a replica of the ancient city of Babylon as the men emerged behind them.

"Wo ist es?" The gunman's voice was harsh and threatening now.

"Diesen Weg, bitte." Christoph's tone was placating, and Morgan guessed he would have to take the men around to where they had been standing only seconds before.

The group walked in front of the table.

Jake tensed behind her, readying himself if they needed to fight.

Morgan held her breath as they passed and she heard the

brush of one man's shoes on the stone by her head.

So close.

"Hier. Schau." The relief in Christoph's voice was palpable as he must have realized they'd moved. But they would be seen easily if the men turned around.

Morgan looked up. The dark corridor was only meters away.

They would have to sprint for it, and she only hoped the men were more concerned with the bricks than with following them. She reached back and squeezed Jake's hand, letting him know to be ready.

She peeked under the table. The men gathered around the inscription and the man with the bag unzipped it, revealing power tools inside.

Morgan ducked low and ran into the darkness, Jake right behind her.

"Scheisse!" A voice rang out in the hall behind them and then the pinging of bullets on stone echoed through the corridor. Morgan raced away down the south wing, along the edge of the Processional Way, past stelae and cuneiform tablets, winged statues with curled beards looking down as they passed.

"Sie waren nur Studenten," Christoph pleaded, his voice fainter now. *They're only students.*

Morgan could only hope the men believed him.

"This way," Jake whispered and they ducked down a side corridor towards a fire exit. They charged through the door and out into the dawn.

As they ran through the streets away from the museum, Morgan wondered what was so important about the inscription. Why were the men so desperate to take it?

CHAPTER 5

Grand Canyon Snake Valley Retreat, USA

SAM'S PHONE BUZZED IN the balmy night. He unwound himself from Lilith's sleeping form and padded out to the deck to take the call.

"I've sent pictures." Krait, his second-in-command, was gruff as ever. "That should be all you need. If you want the actual bricks, we're gonna have to tear them out the wall. I've got myself a hostage in case we need more time so I can do it, but we'll have to hurry."

"Give me a minute to check the resolution." Sam could barely contain his excitement. Finally, they were so close.

He ended the call and went to his wall screen, logged onto his secure email and opened the images that Krait had sent. The brilliant blue of the Ishtar Gate bricks filled the screen, a series of strange dots superimposed over them. Then the other brick was revealed. A cuneiform inscription he had never seen before.

He called Krait back. "It's enough. Get out of there and wait for me to call with where to head next."

Sam padded back into the bedroom and gently shook Lilith's shoulder. She opened her eyes and smiled up at him, a languid look of satisfaction on her face from their earlier time together. He bent to kiss her and her tongue flickered over his lips. Part of him wanted to take her again. But there was something far more important for them to do now.

"It's time," he whispered.

She gasped, her eyes widening in anticipation of the venom he had withheld.

"I have a room prepared." Sam handed Lilith a robe to tie about her naked body. "Come."

The sanctuary sat at the very corner of the lodge, with a wall of glass that gave a 180-degree view over the Canyon and a ceiling that opened to the stars above. The lights were dim and as they walked in, Lilith sensed something else there.

She smiled as she heard the soft rattle.

All around them in the walls were snakes in individual habitats. A desert striped whipsnake, a common king and a beautiful wandering garter snake. She would enjoy handling these another time, but right now she craved the venom trance.

Lilith sat on a pile of cushions facing the open glass wall, looking out towards the Canyon. She settled herself, taking long, deep breaths to prepare.

"The shamans call it spirit walking," she said. "Others call it astral projection."

Sam nodded as he prepared the dose, drawing the inland taipan venom up into the syringe. Lilith watched the level fill, higher than she had ever taken before. It would be intoxicating.

Or it would kill her.

She bit her lip in anticipation, speaking softly to calm herself.

"Each time I've seen things I couldn't know of, visited places I've never traveled to. Each time I hear the voice of the Great Serpent more clearly."

Sam turned to her. "I believe you," he whispered. "Hear him now. Find him so we can bring him back to his rightful place."

He walked towards her with the syringe.

"I prefer to administer it myself," Lilith said softly. He nodded and laid it down gently next to her on a tray. He placed the images from the museum by her side and she fixed those images into her mind. Sam moved back into the shadows, out of her line of sight.

Lilith waited, breathing in the night air, letting her mind reach out into the world of reptilian awareness.

In the moments before she injected, she always questioned her motives. There was a great tradition of mithridatism and her purest reason was surely pragmatic. As a scientist, she worked with snakes and inoculating herself against a possible bite was practical. She had survived once, but that didn't guarantee she would make it through next time. The little death of each tiny shot was protecting her future.

But she knew it was more than that now.

She no longer denied her addiction, but how else was she to rip through the veil to the other side of perception? How else could she tear the world from her eyes and see clearly? This physical realm was just one part of the whole and the venom pierced it.

In the beginning, the serpent tempted Eve with fruit from the Tree of the Knowledge of Good and Evil. This was her temptation even now, for when she took the venom, she saw beyond reality.

She put on the tourniquet, tightened it and quickly injected herself, dropping the needle. It clanged in the tray. Sam let out a sharp intake of breath behind her and moved forward to help. Lilith put out a hand to motion him away.

She shut her eyes, wanting to feel every second of the rush.

The burn was hot, stinging, right on the fulcrum of pleasure and pain. The venom shot through her, spreading like fire through her veins. Everywhere it touched became as molten gold. Her blood sang. She was on fire as the heat curled through her belly, down to her sex.

Lilith began to undulate on the cushions, her hips writhing as she felt the serpent rise within her, taking control of her body. She lay back on the cushions and looked up at the stars, her mind expanding into the night sky above.

Then she felt His touch upon her.

The Serpent of Serpents called her name with a deep longing. She tilted her head to hear Him better as He told her of what she must do. His sibilant hiss vibrated inside her skull as she flew out of her body into the stars. Her breath was forced from her chest as the air rushed past.

Then she was diving back down towards an ocean, drawn forwards by a mysterious force.

She plunged down into the waves, cold seeping into her skin as she felt herself inhabit the body of a sea snake. She was drawn down into the violence of the deep, passing creatures that preyed on the unsuspecting. As the water darkened, she saw bioluminescence, winking lights of anglerfish and dragonfish predators.

A five-foot-long frilled shark buzzed past, baring its rows of razor-sharp, three-pronged teeth. A living fossil, the eel-like shark was rarely seen. Lilith shivered as it passed and she continued down into the abyssal zone.

Deeper still, a dumbo octopus swam past, its ear-like fins swiveling towards her. Part of Lilith's conscious mind logged how deep she was. This creature was considered an extremophile, one of those that lived at extreme depths of over 10,000 feet below the sea.

A plume of what looked like smoke caught her eye as it erupted only meters away. A black smoker, a hydrothermal vent spewing out superheated water.

Near it, she saw something rectangular. It looked manmade in this alien environment and she felt a jolt of recognition.

Then something flashed from the dark.

Lilith saw a long snout like a rhino's horn and rows of nail-like teeth. A goblin shark. The creature rushed towards her, teeth bared, and she pulled out of the trance, panting and sweating.

She was suddenly back in her body, back in the lodge, back in the air above the canyon. She shivered uncontrollably as she gulped air into her lungs. Lilith hugged her arms around herself, trying to warm her skin after the experience of submersion.

Sam knelt next to her and pulled her close. "It's OK. You're back now." He rocked her back and forth and rubbed her arms until her shivering subsided. He helped her to drink a little water as she recovered.

"How long was I out?" she whispered.

Sam glanced at his watch. "Nearly two hours. I was worried."

Lilith turned to him, saw the concern in his eyes. "You needn't have been. I heard His voice. He led me to the depths. He's ready to emerge."

"Where?"

"Deep in the ocean. I recognized some of the species, so we should be able to triangulate the position using the museum images as a starting point. I need to check."

Sam handed her his tablet computer. Lilith searched Google for the marine creatures she had seen.

"Definitely the Pacific." She paused, then tapped away on the screen again. She felt certainty settle within her and then smiled. She opened the Maps application, turning it so Sam could see.

"There. The Mariana Trench, the deepest part of the ocean."

Sam nodded, and she saw no doubt in his eyes.

"Ready yourself," he said, pulling out his phone. "We'll leave as soon as we can."

* * *

Berlin, Germany.

As first light dawned, Morgan and Jake found a park and hunkered down behind a closed coffee shop. Jake video-called Marietti while Morgan sent the picture of the bricks to the Director and Martin.

"We were interrupted," Jake said when they connected. "Another group arrived, men with guns. We couldn't stop them, but we got a picture of an unusual inscription. Morgan's sending it over now."

"I'll get Martin working on it." Marietti frowned. "Did you see this other group?"

"One of the men looked like he'd had a stroke," Morgan said. "He also had a snake tattoo winding around his neck with green and red scales."

"We'll search the criminal databases for him." Then Marietti frowned, recalling a memory. "I knew of a man with a similar tattoo once, but the scales were green and yellow." The Director shook his head with regret. "He was one of us once, but terrorists took him in Africa while on a mission, tortured him under the influence of hallucinogenic drugs. After he stumbled out of the desert and made it back, he was a broken man and resigned from ARKANE. He calls himself Samael, although back when we worked together, he had another name."

"Samael means Venom or Poison of God," Morgan said. "An archangel from Talmudic scripture, a seducer and a destroyer, considered both good and evil." She paused. "Also known as the Angel of Death."

"Indeed," Marietti said. "In the Kabbalah, Samael was said to be the serpent who tempted Eve, who seduced her and fathered Cain. He then became the consort of Lilith, Adam's first wife, and had demon children with her."

"Happy families indeed," Jake said.

"Wait a minute," Marietti said. "I'm going to get Martin in on the call."

Martin came on the line, his shock of blonde hair standing up in clumps. He had a tendency to pull it as he thought. And he did a lot of thinking.

"I've checked this second inscription from the gate against the database. I'm still checking the locational data, but it's brought back something else I can't understand."

Morgan heard confusion in his voice, which was strange because Martin had designed the ARKANE database, hacking into the world's most secret archives to cross-reference across cultures, religions, languages, and even time. There was little he couldn't find out.

"There's only one other example of this image I can find. An unusual destination indeed."

CHAPTER 6

Western Pacific Ocean, above the Mariana Trench.

A BANK OF CLOUD FORMED a dark curtain on the horizon, turning the ocean to ink.

"We have to turn back," the captain said. He gestured at the weather report. It showed a gigantic storm approaching from the northeast. "It's too dangerous. We can't deploy the ROV in this. We're heading back."

Sam turned and nodded to one of his bodyguards. The man pulled a cell phone from his pocket, thumbed a few buttons and then turned the screen. The captain paled at the sight.

"No," he whispered.

"Your wife and son will be fine as long as you help us find what we're looking for," Sam said. "They haven't been hurt … so far. If you help us, you'll be able to retire on the cash bonus. But turn back now, and my men will gut your family like the fish you ate last night."

The captain nodded slowly. "Then we have to hurry. I need the coordinates."

"Start preparing for a dive," Sam said. "I'll get what you need."

* * *

Lilith sat at the very top of the boat, above the captain's deck. There was a private viewing area up here with reinforced glass that gave a 360-degree view of the ocean. As the research vessel rolled with the gigantic waves, the room dipped towards the water, swaying back and forth. She had sat here for the whole trip so far, hearing the hiss of the Great Serpent in the sound of the waves. They were getting closer, she could feel it.

She remained in a state of trance, a light edge of intoxication but Sam carefully monitored her dose. If she could just get hold of the vial …

As a scientist, Lilith understood that venom blocked the acetylcholine receptors in the brain to produce an altered state of consciousness. But the mechanism for how it worked no longer concerned her. It was a drug, pure and simple, and she craved the insight it brought her. Each time the venom entered her bloodstream, she was catapulted into another realm, her senses heightened to exquisite perception.

She heard Sam's footsteps on the stair and her heart beat faster in anticipation. She wanted his touch on her skin, but she craved the venom high even more.

"It's time." He entered the cabin, bracing himself with the handrails against the roll of the boat.

"I'm ready," she said.

He prepared the dose, triple what she had taken before. Lilith knew it was a risk, but she snatched it from him, injecting herself and then lying back with a sigh as her mind took flight.

* * *

Lilith's eyelids flickered and it seemed to Sam that the woman behind the green eyes disappeared. She swayed, her head tipping back as the venom took hold. She shuddered, first gently, then with violent convulsions that turned into writhing.

Had he given her too much this time?

Sam put more cushions around her to contain her movements. Moments later, she began to calm.

Then her mouth opened and she hissed, a low sound that vibrated through Sam's chest.

"Ssssouthwest," she whispered. "See the signs."

Sam wanted more, something that might help further. But Lilith's body sagged and she collapsed unconscious. That was all he was going to get from her right now. But it was enough to get them started.

Sam brushed Lilith's hair back from her face. Her skin was smoother somehow, with the pearlescent look ... of scales, perhaps. He pushed away his guilt at what Lilith was becoming and left her prone on the cushions. He would come back up later to see if she was alright. He only hoped she would survive the dose. After all, he would need her again soon. He would not risk his own life, even to channel the Great Serpent.

Back down in the captain's cabin, the rain hammered on the windows, a staccato beat above the throb of the engine. Sam watched as the crew launched the small Remote Operated Vehicle with a splash into the white-capped waves.

"The little one's fastest," the captain said coldly. "If we find anything, we'll send down the Big Boy to bring it up. Ted here'll be your guide to the deep." He turned his back on Sam, pointedly ignoring him.

Ted, the ROV pilot, sat close to the screen. He used a joystick and manual controls to drive the ROV through the water as it submerged.

"The water is almost as cold as ice further down," he said, "but then there are hydrothermal vents that shoot out superheated water close to 700 degrees Fahrenheit. The black smokers belch minerals from the core of the earth, but the water can't boil because of the water pressure down there, over 155 times that of the surface. There are creatures living in that hell, thriving on the extremities of what we thought possible."

"Like what?" Sam asked, as he scanned the screen for anything that could be considered a sign. What the hell did Lilith's words even mean?

"Like these awesome giant amoebas, xenophyophores, the size of a man's fist. There's millions of them, like the zombie horde." Ted's enthusiasm bubbled over. "There's an underwater volcano too, with a full-on lake of molten sulfur. It's such a cool place."

"There may be even more than you know about down here," Sam said quietly.

Minutes passed into hours and Ted fell silent as the ROV camera saw nothing in the water column except the occasional deep-water prawn and jellyfish.

The darkness of the storm encroached and the captain finally snapped. "We have to get back. How long do you want to watch the emptiness go by?"

Sam whipped around, a snarl on his face. "As long as it takes, old man. Think of your precious family and wait, or I will take their eyes for your impudence."

"Oh, my. Look at this." Ted's voice was tinged with awe. "I've never seen anything like it."

Sam turned back to see the screen filled with writhing sea snakes of all colors, dancing in the water, undulating together. Their heads all faced towards the deep.

"This is more than weird," Ted said. "They shouldn't even be around here. They're solitary creatures but this is like a swarm. Oh man, this is so cool."

"Follow them down," Sam said.

Ted pushed the joystick forward and the ROV dived amongst the writhing snakes, moving faster into the deep. There were thousands of them, tiny ones that darted in front of the camera and huge, thick, long ones that slowly headed deeper.

"Holy crap," Ted said as he watched the fathometer reading. "I've never taken her down this far."

"Keep going."

Minutes later, they reached a seamount covered in writhing serpents, the dying snakes convulsing on top of the already dead, a sacrifice to the deep.

"What are they doing? What's attracted them here?" Ted wondered aloud.

"Take the ROV closer," Sam said. "There's something on top."

As they drew closer, the outline of a large rectangular shape could be seen. It was still covered by piles of snakes, but through the gaps between their bodies, Sam could see what looked like stone.

"Bring it up." The voice from the door was cold and clear.

Sam turned to see Lilith standing there, her green eyes fixed on the screen, her titian hair loose about her face. The silk dress she wore was moulded to her body and as she walked towards them, it was as if she undulated like the sea serpents in the depths. She exuded sex appeal and Sam felt a tightening in his groin. He wanted her, and he could tell by the way Ted shifted uncomfortably on his seat that he felt the attraction too.

But there was also something terrifying about her eyes. They were cold as emeralds, the pupils narrowed to almost vertical slits.

Snake eyes.

"Do what she says," Sam snapped at the captain.

The crew hurried to launch the bigger ROV with grabber arms that would attach balloons that could lift even the heaviest of deep-sea discoveries.

Ted attached the mini ROV to the rectangular object and then piloted the larger vessel down to meet it. He attached balloons to the corners, then manipulated the controls. The balloons began to inflate.

Slowly, the object lifted from the seamount.

The dead snakes fell away, revealing the shape of a sarcophagus, a massive stone box covered in encrusting life and the sludge of the deep. As it rose, slime dripped off it to pool in the waters below.

The captain came to stand close to the screen. "Are you sure we should bring that up here?" he whispered.

"Yesss, it's time." Lilith fixed her green eyes on the man.

He gulped and backed away. "I'll ready the deck for cargo."

The sarcophagus ascended slowly from the deep ocean but, finally, broke the surface by the side of the boat, held up and buffered by the balloons. The waves were high now, the storm almost upon them. The crew battled the driving rain and rolling movement to attach a winch and drag it onto the deck.

The ancient stone was covered in pelagic sediment, a mustard-yellow viscous ooze composed of shells, animal skeletons and decaying organisms that had sunk down to the bottom of the ocean. It smelled of sulfur and rotten fish and the stink of dead snake carcasses. Sam covered his face, trying not to gag as he bent to it. He could just make out carvings under the sediment, twisting in the undulating curves of a serpent. He had waited so long for this, but now he was apprehensive. The next steps were unknown.

Lilith stood grasping the boat's rail in just her thin dress, oblivious to the cold, her eyes fixed on the casket. As powerful waves crashed onto the deck, she walked forward and gently placed her hands on it.

She bent and laid her head upon it, eyes closed, her left ear pressed to the ancient stone, as she listened for something within. Sam marveled to watch her so transformed, so self-assured in the face of the chaos around them.

After a minute, she stood upright again, her dress soaked through, revealing her slender frame. The wind whipped her hair about her face, her green eyes a reflection of the dark ocean around them. She was beyond a woman now, Sam realized.

She was a goddess.

For a moment, he doubted his purpose. He had thought he could use her to find the power he sought, but now he wondered who was really in control.

Suddenly she stumbled, her legs wobbly on the rolling deck. He went to her and grasped her arm. Her skin was freezing, goose-bumped from the chill water.

"It's quiet inside," she whispered in her own voice, her eyes suddenly normal again. "I can't hear him."

"We need to get the casket back to shore," Sam said. "You can take the venom again then." He led her away from the sarcophagus as the men on deck moved to strap it down for the trip home. "Come, rest now. Sleep, and soon we'll be home."

Lilith leaned against him and he half-carried her into their cabin, helping her out of her wet clothes and into bed. Her naked body glistened as she turned away to sleep. Behind her neck, just below her hairline, he saw scales. He brushed her hair over them and stroked her forehead.

"Sleep now," he whispered. She gave a half smile as her breathing shifted into unconsciousness.

* * *

As the captain steered towards home, finally heading out of the storm, Sam went back out on deck. He walked to the sarcophagus and put his ear to the stone. He could hear nothing but the whoosh of the ocean beneath the boat, the slap of the rain on the deck and the engine motor. But there had to be something inside. The prophecy foretold it.

He had to be sure.

He brushed away the remaining dead snakes that hung on the edge of the sarcophagus, and then scraped the stone free of algae along the top half. There were indentations along the edge, carvings reminiscent of cuneiform and underneath, what looked like Greek.

He scraped the pelagic sediment from the front of the sarcophagus, needing to be sure. The Roshite scriptures told of a seal that would unlock the burial chamber. He pulled a small ebony box from his pocket, carved with the whorls of a coiled snake. It had been passed down for generations, believed to be the seal. He opened it and lifted the amulet out, checking the carvings on it with those on the sarcophagus.

His heart beat faster and a smile spread across his lips as he found, with relief, that they were the same. This was indeed the resting place of the Serpent of Serpents.

But as he brushed away the remnants of the deep, Sam found that there were seven indentations in the stone, each with a separate carving.

He had only one seal. So where were the others?

He headed inside to call Krait. It was time for the next phase.

BBC NEWS REPORT

THE SPATE OF EXTREME weather conditions across the globe continues this morning. The most powerful hurricane to hit Florida in living memory made landfall last night, leaving hundreds of thousands with no power and several hundred people dead.

In Taiwan, a super-typhoon lashed the coast, destroying property and causing chaos at airports.

In New Zealand, aftershocks continue to pummel the North Island after an earthquake measuring 7.1 on the Richter scale occurred deep off the northeast coast.

In Ecuador, a double earthquake has left thousands dead and many thousands more homeless as aid workers scramble to reach those affected. And in Great Britain, more than one hundred flood warnings have been issued as torrential rain and flooding pummel the country.

Some are taking the strange weather as a sign of the times, pointing to the imminent End of Days. Pastor Louis Masterson of Tallahassee stood on the steps of his church in ankle-deep water, palm trees whipping about his head, as he spoke to reporters. "As Luke's gospel, chapter twenty-one says, there will be strange signs in the sun, moon and stars. And here on earth, the nations will be in turmoil perplexed by roaring seas and strange tides."

As politicians call for calm, scientists explain the confluence of freak weather events as being due to a series of super moons combined with an incredibly rare lunar cycle.

CHAPTER 7

Ouidah, Benin.

MORGAN SHIELDED HER EYES against the bright sun as the *zemidjan* motorbike-taxi sped through the outer limits of the city. Tamarind and jasmine trees lined the streets. People walked along the dusty roadside, deftly avoiding the motorbikes and stray dogs as they headed for the central market. Only a few days ago, she and Jake had been back in Africa, further east in Rwanda, and now they were both in this sliver of a country in French West Africa.

Here in Ouidah, the landscape was marked by a dark past. The oldest area of the city was filled with the elegantly crumbling architecture of empire, the relics of wealth built on the backs of slaves. They passed an eighteenth-century Portuguese fort built to administer the slave trade, and several grand Afro-Brazilian houses built by emancipated slaves. Those lucky few who made it back from the Americas.

"This was once the Route des Esclaves, the Slave Route," the taxi driver explained, clearly used to ferrying tourists around. "You can still trace the final walk made by thousands of slaves to the coast of the Atlantic Ocean. There was once a Tree of Forgetfulness here. The slaves would walk around it nine times in order to forget their old life and family, so they could be happy in their new life across the ocean."

They drove on to a desolate beach fringed by palm trees

on the edge of the Gulf of Guinea, where a gigantic arch stood in shades of ochre, black and white.

"The Door of No Return," the driver said. "The last stage of the journey to slavery."

Morgan felt an urge to look at the monument more closely. "Can we stop a minute?" she asked.

"Of course, it is a sacred place."

The driver pulled over and waited as they got out. Jake wandered away, silent with his own thoughts. Morgan took off her shoes to feel the sand under her feet as those chained would have done before boarding the ships. So many died on the way over, the rest dying across the ocean, far from those they loved. She looked up. On the top of the arch, chained slaves marched towards stylized ships with heads bowed. On each side of the memorial, voodoo gods stood to welcome the souls of dead slaves back to their homeland.

Morgan looked out at the ocean, the waves turquoise in the shallows and darkening towards the horizon. The air smelled of salt and fish caught and processed further down the coast. Tears pricked at her eyes as she considered the many thousands taken from here to bleed and die on foreign soil.

Of course, it was unthinkable to unravel how history might have panned out if the evil of the slave trade had not happened at all. Like much of man's inhumanity to man, once events had been set in motion, the resulting effects echoed through history. The Shoah – the Holocaust – had the same resonance for Jews. Without Hitler's abomination, would there be a modern state of Israel? Without the slave trade, would there have been a black President of the USA?

Morgan felt an echo of her own history here, a people uprooted from their homes and treated like animals across the seas. But when she returned to Israel, she felt it was her home. She wondered how the diaspora Beninese felt when they came back generations after slavers took their ancestors to the Americas. There had also been native people here who were complicit in the slave trade, tribes raiding other tribes for slaves to trade with the westerners. Like the *capos*, Jews who helped guard the death camps. Just as in the rest of life, there was good and bad on both sides. No race came out with completely clean hands.

One of the resulting effects of the slave trade had been the transplant of voodoo beliefs to Haiti and Brazil, and Morgan felt the throb of those vibrant cultures here. Voodoo was the state religion in Benin, followed by sixty percent of Beninese. In Haitian voodoo, Damballa, the creator loa, was represented by a serpent and there were water loa in serpentine form. Morgan wondered what they would find in the city of Ouidah.

They got back in the taxi and drove into the town. They passed Zomachi, the Remembrance monument, built in 1998, part of a ceremony to ask forgiveness from God for the sins of the ancestors who aided in slavery.

Eventually, they stopped on the edge of the market. Morgan leaned out as they passed a voodoo stall to look at a pile of ritual objects. The air reeked of decomposition and a musty dryness. She tried to work out what she was looking at.

Suddenly, Jake screwed up his nose. "Oh, no. That's a hippo foot. Gross."

Once she realized they were animal parts, Morgan could make out a dog's head, what looked like a pickled chameleon, and a crocodile snout, all used in voodoo ceremonies.

"But no snakes," Morgan noted. "We have to go further."

They finally arrived outside the entrance of the Python temple. Morgan had been expecting something grand and ornate, like the Indian Hindu temples, but the bricks were plain, a muted pink with white panels. *Temple des pythons* was painted in blue and red over the metal doorway, and she could see simple huts with straw roofs inside the compound.

The driver pointed behind the temple to trees beyond.

"Hundreds of years ago, King Kpassè of Ouidah was defeated in a war and he fled to the forest to escape those who came to capture him. The Royal Pythons saved him and in their honor, he built the temple here and another beyond in the forest. The python represents the voodoo god Dan, and people here will not kill a python for fear of bad luck striking them." He smiled and waved them towards the gate. "I will leave you here. May the blessings of the Great Serpent be upon you."

Morgan and Jake paid the driver and walked into the compound. Three huts with painted doors flanked a central open area, each door propped open to provide a glimpse of the snake pits within. In the center was a sacred Iroko tree, under which a couple of pythons curled, languid in the heat of the day. A man sat in the shade of one of the huts, relaxing under a straw awning that kept the strong sun off his head.

And off the python curled around his shoulders.

He looked up at them with curiosity in his eyes as they entered, but he didn't move. He just nodded and Morgan returned his greeting with a smile. The man fingered a set of *Fa* beads, threads of eight wooden disks, just as a Catholic would count his rosary. But Morgan knew that the *Fa* beads could be cast and the positions read to interpret the will of the gods. Mediums channeled spirits here in Benin, and possession was almost normal during worship. The supernatural was part of everyday life.

They walked into one of the round huts. It was dark and smelled musty. The sound of slithering over straw came from the pit in the center. As Morgan's eyes adjusted to the dark, she could see the pythons that lay on the steps around them, a few on the top levels and more in the pit below.

Jake stayed near the door.

"They look pretty chilled," he said. "So what exactly are we looking for?"

"Something that looks similar to the image from the Ishtar Gate." Morgan walked around the outside of the pit, her hands running over the smooth walls. Jake walked in the opposite direction, both of them checking for any hidden niches. But the walls were plain and smooth. There wasn't even an altar. Perhaps they offered food directly to the snakes, Morgan thought, glancing into the pit.

She wasn't scared of snakes particularly, but she had no desire to get any closer if they didn't have to. They walked back round to the doorway.

"Perhaps we should –"

Morgan's words were interrupted by voices shouting from outside.

A gunshot. A sharp howl of grief.

They ducked down and Morgan looked around the edge of the door. In the courtyard, four men stood with guns trained on the old man who sat in the shade. One of the pythons lay unmoving before him, blood seeping from its body.

The leader of the group was the man with the snake tattoo she had seen in Berlin.

And there was no way out of this room.

"Where are they?" the tattooed man said, his voice brusque as he addressed the old Beninese in English, then in French. "Qui est là? Où se cachent-ils?"

"He's asking where we're hiding," Morgan breathed in Jake's ear, and she saw his own concern matched hers.

They only had seconds before they were discovered.

A snake caught Morgan's eye as it moved within the deep pit, writhing over the others. There were holes in the sides of the pit, cool alcoves for the serpents to hide in when the sun became too high.

"Are you really sure that you're over your snake phobia?" Morgan whispered.

Jake followed her gaze to the pit of snakes. "I guess we're going to find out."

They heard the old man talking as they clambered down into the pit. "Je pourrais savoir. Je pourrais pas savoir." *I might know. I might not know.*

Then the sound of the *Fa* beads cast upon the earth. Morgan realized that he was asking the spirits for direction.

In her concentration on the sounds, she narrowly missed putting her hand on a python's head. It hissed, flickering its tongue at her, tasting her passing.

Jake placed his feet gingerly between the coils, heading for one of the alcoves out of direct sight of the door. He seemed to be doing OK so far, but then he wasn't lying in a confined space with the snakes yet. Morgan was acutely aware that he had almost died the last time she'd gotten him involved with snakes. She hoped he was right about being healed in New York.

A moment later, the old man's voice came again.

"Il n'y a personne pour vous ici."

There's no one here for you. He wasn't giving away their position, but it was a small compound and the men could still find them soon enough.

Moving slowly so as not to disturb the snakes too much, Morgan knelt down and then lowered herself to lie flat, curling around the serpents that were already down there. Jake was in the alcove next to her, his face white, sweat pooling on his brow. His eyes were wide. All the hallmarks of fear.

"They're pythons," she whispered. "They shouldn't bite you."

"Just squeeze me to death." He mouthed the words and Morgan smiled. He was clearly managing.

They both lay flat, easing into the alcove as the sound of men searching came from above. Morgan heard footsteps. Then the sound of breathing from the lip of the pit.

CHAPTER 8

MORGAN IMAGINED THE MAN looking down into the pit. If he caught a glimpse of them, they'd be easy targets.

And if Jake freaked out, they'd be caught for sure.

"A lot of damn snakes, but there's no one in here," the man called from above, his voice getting softer as he walked away towards the door. Then the scuff of boots as another man joined him.

"Samael will be properly mad if we don't find the second seal. It must be here somewhere."

Morgan frowned. The second seal? That implied they had one already and there were more to be found.

"Il y a un autre temple." The voice of the old Beninese filtered down from the courtyard. "Dans la foret. Là bas."

He must be pointing them to another temple in the forest behind. She and Jake would have time to escape if the men went looking.

Moments later, the footsteps receded. The men were gone.

Morgan and Jake slid from their respective alcoves. Jake wasn't sweating any longer, and he even stroked one of the pythons with a bemused smile as they clambered out. Morgan wondered anew what had happened in New York, but it seemed that whatever it was, it had worked. And for that, she was grateful.

They tiptoed to the edge of the hut and peered around. The courtyard was empty except for the old man sitting in the shade, looking down at the *Fa* beads in the dirt in front of him.

He turned his head and beckoned to them, the other hand still stroking the python that curled around his shoulders.

"Les esprits me disent de vous montrer quelque chose. Viens."

"He says that the spirits have told him to show us something," Morgan said, as they walked back across the courtyard.

The old man pulled himself upright and lifted the serpent from his shoulders, laying it gently on the ground in the shade. He shuffled ahead of them to a scruffy prefab building, what looked like a maintenance shed in the corner of the compound.

He pushed open the door and beckoned them again.

They followed him in and he pointed to the corner of the dirt-floored hut.

"Creuser," he said, motioning a digging action.

Jake raised an eyebrow at Morgan and picked up a spade that stood propped against the wall. After digging down a few inches, he struck metal. He looked up for permission. The old man nodded.

Jake dug his fingers into the soft dirt and pulled out a metal box. Something rattled inside.

He opened it to reveal a round stone carved with intertwined snakes.

"The seal?" Morgan lifted it out, judging its weight. It matched the markings from the Ishtar Gate. It was just three inches in diameter, the perfect size for sealing important documents ... or a sarcophagus.

"Les esprits disent que vous devez prendre cela et aller." The old man glanced behind him at the forest. "Maintenant, et rapidement."

The spirits say to take this and go. Morgan turned to him, the seal in her hand.

"Are you sure? This must be precious to your people."

The man must have understood her expression, if not her words. He put one hand on her head as if to bless her, and with the other, he curled her hand around the seal.

"We should get going," Jake said. "The others will be out of that forest soon if they can't find anything."

"Thank you," Morgan said as they passed the old man at the doorway.

He nodded. As they walked away, Morgan heard him whisper, "Ne me remerciez pas, ma fille. Le sceau est une malédiction et non une bénédiction."

As they left the compound, Jake turned to Morgan.

"What did he say as we left?"

She clutched the seal more tightly as they hailed a taxi. "He said not to thank him. The seal is a curse, not a blessing." She looked up at Jake. "I think this is only the beginning."

* * *

As soon as they reached the airport, Morgan and Jake found a quiet corner and called ARKANE HQ.

As they recounted what had happened at the temple and the man's words, Marietti paled, the color draining from his cheeks. "The Seven Seals. It must be."

"What do you mean?" Jake asked.

"The book of Revelation talks of Seven Seals at the End Times," Morgan said. "As each one is broken, they release terrible things upon the earth, including the Four Horseman of the Apocalypse. Most would say they are allegory, but perhaps they are actually real."

"The seals open the sarcophagus," Marietti said, his voice faint. "The rumored resting place of the Great Serpent, bound for a thousand years."

"But all seven are needed to open it, right?" Jake noted. "So let's get the rest and destroy them before this serpent crew have them all."

Marietti nodded, and then shook his head as if to clear it. "You're right. I was forgetting myself. For so long, we have tried to keep these prophecies from coming true. But in the end, we are but pawns in the long game of eternity. Martin, do you have any leads on the other seals?"

Martin tapped away on the screen. "I've got the database running now, looking for images from ancient civilizations that relate to serpent gods. There are so many, so I'll need to narrow them down."

"Start with those that are closer to Babylon physically," Morgan said. "The Australian Aboriginal people have a creation snake but I can't think that a seal would be hidden so far, millennia before the continent was discovered by westerners."

Martin nodded. "I think I have a place for you to start. Your old stomping ground, Morgan. Considered by many to be the beginning of the End of Days."

* * *

Grand Canyon Snake Valley Retreat, USA

A military helicopter lowered the crate into a massive hole dug into the ground outside the lodge. Wooden slats protected the ancient sarcophagus as it creaked with the strain. Wind whipped the loose earth into flurries around it, obscuring what was within.

Sam's men guided it down into the hole and onto a custom-made trolley. From there, they wheeled it along and down into a specially prepared vault.

Lilith stayed close, her hand resting on its side, her concern like a mother hen for her chicks. She hadn't let it out of her sight on the journey back. She knew something was inside, although that something didn't have a heartbeat and she hadn't heard His voice since the boat.

But then Sam kept the vial of venom close to him and he wouldn't let her have any more until they were sure of the next step. Until he had the other seals.

She glanced over at him as they rolled down the tunnel. He was weak, spineless.

He was not worthy to open the sarcophagus. The serpent had chosen Eve in the Garden of Eden, as He chose Lilith now. The curves of the serpent were her curves. Samael could try to tame the serpent's power, but only she would channel it to glory.

She would have to be careful of Sam, keep him close for now. But in the end, only one of them would stand in front of the Serpent of Serpents.

* * *

Sam noted the change in Lilith's posture as the sarcophagus rolled towards the vault. Her steps became a glide and she hovered close, her hands fluttering near the stone as if protecting something precious. He felt her eyes upon him and the hair on his neck prickled with awareness. Could he still trust her? His hand moved instinctively to the vial within his jacket pocket. As long as he controlled her addiction, he could control her.

His phone buzzed. Krait's name appeared on screen.

Sam turned back down the tunnel to answer the call.

"Someone else was there in Ouidah." Krait's voice was harsh over the line, his anger barely contained. "The seal was taken from under our noses. We returned from the forest empty-handed, clearly sent on a wild goose chase, to find the guardian of the temple gone. There was a hole dug in one of the huts. Something was taken." He paused. "I'm wondering if the supposed students in Berlin were those seeking what we are looking for, too."

Sam frowned. He hadn't considered that others might be on the trail. He had backing from powerful groups affiliated with the Vatican, extremist Islam and fundamentalist Jews. They all had a vested interest in bringing forward the End of Days, so it wouldn't be any of them. There was another organization, though … He'd been expecting them.

ARKANE.

Memories came flooding back and he walked back out into the dust of the mesa to clear his head.

With his Egyptian-American heritage, Sam had been an agent based out of ARKANE's New York office, sent to work undercover in Egypt. His mission had been to infiltrate a cell, part of an antiquities smuggling ring. Powerful relics were being passed to terrorist cells in the Middle East, traded as occult objects believed to have great power in the battles to come. Hitler's elite troops had sought artifacts that would influence the supernatural realm; now, those who sought to expel the US and Britain from the Middle East were seeking the same. Sam had believed he was doing the right thing … until that fateful day.

Sam sighed and touched the locket around his neck. It was hidden under his clothes, a sign of weakness he didn't let others see. He thought of Leila, her smiling face, her dark eyes filled with love. But she was lost to him now, her body broken and buried by a targeted bomb from his own country.

* * *

They had been out in the desert of Libya, having finally been invited to one of the terrorist camps where the exchange of archaeological objects took place. He had been gathering the final evidence needed to take them down.

A high-pitched whistle, screams and then blackness.

Sam's hands shook as he remembered the terror of waking beneath the crushing sand. His rising panic as he couldn't breathe. Clawing his way up to the surface. Screaming for Leila as burned ash rained down on body parts strewn around him.

He hadn't found her remains, but as one of the few survivors and a stranger, he had been swept up by the surviving militants and taken to a camp deeper in the desert.

The torture was sweet punishment after his loss. He longed for death, begging the men, goading them. They injected him with snake venom and during his hallucinogenic visions, he told them whatever they wanted. He roamed the earth above his body in those times, taken higher by the drugs. It was then that he heard the voice of the Great Serpent for the first time.

His captors didn't believe his story of ARKANE and its quest for supernatural artifacts. They wanted American military spies, hostages they could trade, and in the end, men they could behead on video. Another propaganda win in an unequal war.

When they dressed and hooded him, then dragged him to another room, he had expected it to end with the hack of a jagged blade.

But they sliced away his bonds.

When the hood came off, there was only one other man in a room dimly lit with lamps. A tray of sweet mint tea sat in front of him with two small glasses, typical of Arab hospitality.

"Drink," the man said softly. He sat down across from Sam. "Here, I will show you it is fine." He poured two glasses and sipped out of one. "It's good."

Sam reached out a trembling hand. The first sip was

nectar on his parched throat. The man watched him, his dark eyes interested but patient. When the tea was finished, he called for more.

"In the depths of your torture, you called for Leila." The man pulled a phone from his pocket and showed a picture. "Is this her?"

Sam felt tears prick and his voice wavered. "Yes. She died in the drone attack."

"A drone attack by the US government." The man's words were matter of fact. "Your government."

Sam lifted his chin. "I'm half-Egyptian. My father always talked of home, but he was driven out by extremists. So to whom am I meant to be loyal?"

The man chuckled and shook his head. "We live in mixed-up times. Migration and inter-marriage make us all brothers and sisters and yet we still tell stories of murder and injustice by the Other." He leaned forward. "But you are not who we thought you were. The hallucinogens we gave you were based on snake venom. I've used it in smaller quantities myself for the journey trance, but you were able to take much higher doses."

The man reached for his phone again and played a snippet of sound. Sam heard his own voice, or what sounded like his voice, but it hissed and spat.

"It isss time. The Great Serpent awakes. Ssseek his resting place."

"What does it mean?" Sam asked, even as he felt a deep resonance within him, a desire to heed the voice.

The man took a deep breath and grasped Sam's hand. "The thousand years are ended."

* * *

A night bird called and Sam found himself back in the mesa on the edge of the Grand Canyon. The wind rustled through the rocky landscape and the chirp of the cicadas anchored him back to the land. That long night of discovery in the Libyan desert had led to this day. If only his mentor Farid had lived to see it. But the Brotherhood of the Serpent now awaited his word, for if the Great Serpent emerged, the End of Days would be ushered in.

The world would be remade.

ARKANE couldn't stop him now because the seals were in reach. Their organization was weak, pathetic, nothing in the face of the powerful allies he had. There were only a few places where the seals could be. He would send Krait to the next location to intercept them.

CHAPTER 9

Israel.

MORGAN SMILED AS SHE and Jake drove north from Tel Aviv along the coast road. The air smelled of salt from the Mediterranean Sea and the fresh scent of pine trees. The sky was blue above and she relished the sun on her face. After the flight from Benin, it felt good to be in control of how they traveled. She pressed down on the accelerator of the two-seater convertible, reveling in the speed and the wind in her hair. She felt at home in England now, but when she returned to Israel, she knew this place would always be the closest to her heart.

After their parents divorced when she was little, her twin sister Faye had remained in England with their Christian mother, and Morgan had been brought up here in Israel with their Jewish father. The twin sisters were close now and Morgan loved her niece Gemma deeply. But she knew that Faye would never understand the part of her that was Israeli, the part that thrilled to be out in the desert, to be on the knife-edge of conflict and to be part of a history that still played out its daily ritual of blood vengeance. England was undoubtedly safer, but Morgan felt more alive here. Her father was gone now, buried in a graveyard further north in Safed, the Kabbalah heart of Israel, but she still had friends here. She still felt the throb of history in every kilometer they drove.

"Happy to be back?" Jake said from the passenger seat, as he leaned his head back to catch more sun.

"Surprisingly so," Morgan said. "I know it was a little crazy last time we were here." In the hunt for the Key to the Gates of Hell, they had criss-crossed Israel, even diving in the depths of the Dead Sea before Jake had been evacuated from the salt pillars of Sodom in the Negev desert further south. "But hopefully there'll be less shooting this time around."

"So tell me about Megiddo," Jake said. "Why is Martin so sure that there's a seal there?"

"First of all, it's the biblical Armageddon," Morgan replied. "The site of the final battle in the End Times, described in Revelation chapter sixteen. The archaeological dig there has found twenty-six layers of ruins, so it's likely the apocalyptic reputation comes from the number of times it was destroyed and rebuilt due to its strategic location."

They turned off the main highway, heading east towards Nazareth.

"But it's what they've found in the excavations that we're here to see. Serpent cult objects from the Bronze Age, when snakes were used as part of the Canaanite religion."

The sun was low in the sky by the time they drove into the Jezreel Valley and on to the kibbutz at Megiddo, past olive and citrus trees that filled the air with a fresh scent. There was a bigger settlement nearby but they were staying in the more original housing, kept for tourists who wanted a taste of how kibbutznik had lived in the early days of the state of Israel. This particular kibbutz had been founded in 1949 by Holocaust survivors from Hungary and Poland.

A young woman walked out of the guest accommodation as they pulled up. Her long brown legs peeked out of denim shorts and she had a red checked shirt tied around her waist. Her dark hair hung loose around her face, and Morgan caught a glimpse of her own younger days. She and her husband Elian had spent many happy nights up here in the north, when he was off duty from fighting at the front and she could get away from her job as a military psychologist for the Israeli Defense Force.

Their nights had been filled with feasting and song and laughter and they had thought they would live forever. But Elian had died in a hail of bullets in the Golan Heights, defending the country they both loved. Would he even recognize her now? Morgan wondered. She had changed so much since joining ARKANE, and her beliefs and loyalties had been challenged at every turn. She was a world away from the young woman she had been back then.

But she still loved this land with fierce passion.

She and Jake got out of the car.

"Welcome to our home. I'm Rachel," the young woman said. "I'll be your guide to the Tel."

"Is there time before it gets dark to visit the site?" Morgan asked.

Rachel nodded. "Of course. Your organization called ahead. I've arranged for the snake artifacts to be brought to one of the viewing rooms so we can see them after the dig visit." She smiled. "And of course, you'll want to be back for dinner." The smell of garlic and the sound of sizzling came from the kitchens beyond. "My mother is the chef here. Her Orez Shu'it is to die for."

"White bean stew," Morgan explained to Jake as they grabbed their bags from the car. "You'll love it."

"So let's get over to the dig and then hurry back. My stomach's rumbling already."

They jumped in the back of a battered, dusty truck and Rachel drove them the short distance to the dig.

"The city of Megiddo guarded a narrow pass on the ancient Fertile Crescent," Rachel explained as they parked up by the visitor center. "That's why it was so sought after. There's been a settlement here since the early Bronze Age, around 3500 BC. We've uncovered part of what's considered the largest structure in the Near East, so this was a powerful city."

The sun was setting as they got out of the car and looked out across the Jezreel Valley, the deep green of the lush National Park alive with birdsong.

"Amazing to think of the battles that have been fought here," Jake said, shaking his head. "We think our current empires are so important, but we all disappear with the march of time."

"Megiddo has stood for 5000 years," Rachel said. "Come, I'll show you the main dig before it gets too dark."

She led them down some steps into the dig itself, where a path wound through levels of the city, with plaques indicating the time period of each.

"The city gates would have been here," Rachel said. "This area is called the Ivory Palace, as a significant cache of ancient ivory objects and jewelry were discovered here. Some of them are in the visitor center."

She walked on until they reached a circular pit with a metal staircase attached to one side.

"This shaft goes down twenty-five meters and then extends seventy meters west to the spring that kept the city alive when it was under siege. It's an incredible feat of ancient engineering and enabled the city to survive much longer than others of the area."

A metallic smell came up on the air from the pit, a tang of water deep below. Morgan peered down into the dark. How many feet had descended these stairs, she wondered. Had her ancestors trodden these very paths?

"It's too dark to go down now," Rachel said. "But would you like to see the serpents?"

"Definitely," Jake said.

They walked back to the visitor center and Rachel took them into a special, atmosphere-controlled room. She swiped her security pass against the door and they went in. Two long bronze snakes lay in the center of a white table, their surfaces pockmarked with age. Morgan pulled on a pair of white gloves and picked one up. There was nothing on it that matched the seal. The other one was just as plain.

Disappointment welled within her. "Where were the snakes found?"

"In the Bronze Age stratum." Rachel turned to a replica of the excavations, cut through to show the different sections. "Over here. The dig is still ongoing but there are a number of other objects associated with the serpents, currently undergoing testing."

"We're looking for a round stone, carved like a seal. Have you seen anything like that?"

Rachel frowned as she thought. "I'm not sure, to be honest. The dig is jam-packed with objects from all eras. You can't help falling over things, but I can take you into the research area tomorrow when the curator is back on deck. He doesn't like people in there without him." She smiled ruefully. "He's my PhD supervisor, so I have to stay on his good side."

"Of course," Morgan said, with a sideways glance at Jake. "Tomorrow, then."

They drove back to the camp and joined the kibbutznik around the campfire. They shared a meal together and Morgan enjoyed the camaraderie that stemmed from a country surrounded by enemies, people who worked the land together and turned the desert into bountiful produce. The Orez Shu'it was everything Rachel had promised, chased down with a fruity, full-bodied Syrah from the Golan Heights. There were moments when Morgan forgot the mission and just enjoyed being here with Jake and new friends in the country she didn't live in anymore, but still called home.

* * *

Later, as they headed back to the guest accommodation, Morgan took Jake's arm, walking close to him through the olive grove.

"We can't wait until tomorrow to see if there's a seal in the research area," she whispered. "If it's there, we need to take it and they're hardly going to let us do that during office hours."

Jake nodded. "See you at two a.m., then?" He grinned and the moon caught his corkscrew scar as he turned towards her. "A little night adventure, just the two of us." He pulled Rachel's pass from his back pocket. "This might help."

Morgan smiled. "Good one."

They stopped for a moment and she wanted to lean into him, to feel his hard body against hers. Being back in Israel made her brutally aware of the shortness of life, of how fleeting pleasure could be. And this place, this Armageddon, cast a shadow over her, filling her with a foreboding she couldn't shake.

Morgan pushed the feeling away, and they walked on to the huts.

"See you later," she whispered as they entered the separate rooms.

* * *

In the darkness of the olive grove beyond the camp, Krait stood over the body of an unconscious Israeli guard. The man was bleeding and hog-tied but he'd live. No point in causing an international incident … just yet.

He waited until the two had entered their accommodation and then checked his camera. With a long lens, Krait had shot photos of the pair laughing with the kibbutzniks around the campfire. He knew they had one seal from Benin and he ached to repay the humiliation of that loss. It wouldn't take long to slice their throats in the dark, or maybe he'd spend more time on the woman.

But he had to wait.

Krait emailed the photos to Samael with a text. *They don't have the seal yet, but it's definitely here. Do you want me to take them tonight?*

He sat down in the darkness, one hand on his knife, itching for blood, and waited for the reply.

CHAPTER 10

Grand Canyon Snake Valley Retreat, USA

S A M   L O O K E D   A T   T H E photos Krait had emailed, the
carefree smiles of the two who held one of the seals he
needed. With a word, Krait would finish them tonight and
he would hold the seals by tomorrow, one step closer to
opening the sarcophagus.

They didn't deserve to touch the sacred objects. They
were his by right.

He began to text back, his decision made.

"Ssstop." Lilith's voice was soft but strong. "Let them
find the others." Sam turned abruptly to see her standing
right behind him. He started at how close she had gotten
without him realizing. She had become quieter since they
had returned from the deep and Sam felt a rising concern at
her growing powers.

But Lilith was not the only presence now.

Her green eyes were empty, the pupils dark and slitted
like the snake she had wrapped around her neck, one of the
rock pythons from his terrarium. She stroked it with gentle
fingertips. Had she gotten to the vial of venom? He needed
to be more careful and control her trance states.

"We will take the ssseals when it is time, Samael."

Sam nodded, unsure to whom he spoke. But for now, he
could bide his time.

He deleted the text he'd starting writing to Krait.

Lilith stared at him intently, as if she could read his doubts about her.

Sam typed a new message. *Let them find the seal tonight and then follow them.*

Lilith smiled and slipped away, her body undulating back to the stairs of the vault as she headed back down to the sarcophagus. He imagined her lying across it, her flesh against the cool stone. Part of him wanted to go down there and take her against the casket. He would show her what was real life and what was still just dead stone.

But what if she was channeling the Great Serpent even now?

He banished these darker thoughts and turned back to the pictures of the two ARKANE agents. He would let them find the next few seals, but in the meantime, he would find out who they were … and who they loved. He would not leave the next phase to chance.

* * *

Megiddo, Israel.

The moon was in shadow when Jake heard the light tap on his door. He was ready to go in dark clothes, with a small pack containing a head-torch and tools in case they needed them. He opened the door to see Morgan standing outside, her beautiful face alive with excitement, and he smiled at her enthusiasm. For all their missions together, she still made him feel alive.

The last time they had been in Israel together, he had been poisoned by snake bites in the salt caves of Mount Sodom. His phobia was like another life now. The experience underneath New York really had changed something within. Call it a miracle or merely some kind of psychological shift, it didn't really matter, Jake thought. The result was the same. He could be a worthy partner for Morgan again, and for that, he was grateful.

They walked out into the dark together, easy in their silence, and padded out past the kibbutz towards the Tel. They didn't dare drive in case the noise brought the guards, but Morgan was confident they could pass the night security on foot. This was her land and with her training in the Israeli Defense Force, Jake trusted her to get them back into the archaeological dig without a hitch.

It crossed his mind that Morgan didn't really need him; that she could do all this alone.

But then she reached for his hand in the dark, a moment of connection while the night hid their faces. There was something between them that went beyond just ARKANE partners, something they had come close to acknowledging a number of times, but a relationship was impossible with their dangerous lifestyle. Perhaps they really did need each other, though – not just to watch each other's backs, but to keep the other grounded. After all, the things they saw on ARKANE missions would make the sanest person a little crazy. He squeezed Morgan's hand back, hoping that she could feel what he could never say.

They walked together through the olive groves and onto the road. The air smelled of lemon thyme. Clouds covered the moon. Once they reached the perimeter of the kibbutz, they jogged to the Tel site, slowing as they reached the outer gate. The guards weren't in sight, so Jake swiped Rachel's pass and they went inside, heading straight for the research center that they had skipped past earlier.

At the door, Jake tried the pass again. The light flashed green.

Morgan exhaled with relief and they pushed the door open.

Even though the shutters were closed, they put on headtorches with bulbs dimmed, so as not to attract the guards. It was organized chaos inside, a cornucopia to be explored, much like the dig itself. A number of white plastic boxes were piled on top of one another, each with a separate object inside. Rough handmade clay vessels, each a smaller size as they nested inside one another like an ancient Russian doll. Delicate gold earrings next to a seal ring with a fish etched into it. Rows of tiny beads made of gold, silver and carnelian.

"Hmm." Jake bent to one of the boxes. "There are labels on all these, but they're in Hebrew. I have to admit that mine is a little rusty."

"We can't pull all the boxes apart," Morgan said. "It will be obvious that someone has been here." She looked around at the piles. "But I don't see any other way to find the seal unless there's some kind of index."

"Probably computerized. We could get Martin to hack in?"

"No time," Morgan said. "I guess the other option is just to make it really obvious someone was in here. They're going to discover the seal is missing anyway – if we find it – and the longer we're here, the more chance of discovery." She glanced over to Jake. "Let's just not break anything. There's some serious history in here."

They took half the room each and methodically worked through the trays, moving each out the way to see into the trays beneath. Jake noted that Morgan was slower than he was, distracted by the interesting objects she uncovered. When she had first joined ARKANE, she had been an academic and if he was honest, he hadn't considered her an appropriate partner for missions.

But here they were.

He had underestimated her back then. Now he watched her lean closer to one tray, her fingers reaching out as if to touch something. Her blue eyes, the right with a brilliant violet slash, fixed on the object. Then she felt his gaze and turned to him.

"Have you found something?"

"No." Jake shook his head. "I just like watching you."

A smile played around her lips.

"No time for that now," she said softly. "But come look at this. I think this might be it."

Jake walked closer, aware of her slight curves next to him in the semi darkness. Her head-torchlight played over a grey lump of what looked like hardened clay, the color of storm clouds over water.

With gentle hands, Morgan picked up the clay piece and turned it over. There was a round seal set inside the lump. The carvings were faint, but Jake could make out the undulations of a serpent, a different design from the one they'd found in Benin, but similar enough to be related.

"It certainly looks like the other one," Jake said. "It seems strange that the seals are so far apart, though."

"I love how they're part of a diaspora, just like the Jewish people." Morgan smiled. "These ancient objects are passed down through families who move across the face of the earth, taking their most precious possessions with them. It's not so strange. There's been a trade route into Africa for millennia, and there were great kingdoms there long before Europe rose to power. Remember the Pentecost stones, handed down by the Keepers and spread from Iran all the way to America?"

Jake nodded.

"I think the seals will be spread out, too." Morgan ran her fingertip across the clay around the seal. "If you take Revelation as only part allegory, then someone bound the serpent in a pit. Someone sealed it and then presumably made sure the seals were hidden."

"You really think there's some kind of real serpent in a real pit."

Morgan shrugged. "I didn't believe in the literal Gates of Hell until I saw them with my own eyes. Sometimes that night seems like a dream, like it didn't happen, but in my nightmares I still see the dark wraiths."

Jake thought of what he had seen under New York. "I know what you mean," he whispered. "Let's get out of here."

Morgan wrapped the lump of clay containing the seal in a jersey she'd brought with her and put it in her backpack alongside the other one.

Two down, Jake thought. Not a bad start. The question now was where they would look for the next one.

They left the research hut and headed back through the dig, careful to avoid the guards. Once they were out of hearing range, they could talk freely again.

"I think we should just get up and leave early," Morgan said. "If we go tonight, it will raise suspicion."

Jake nodded. "But if we leave before breakfast, we can say goodbye in a civilized manner and be at the airport by the time the research team gets to work and discovers the seal is gone. Good plan."

They headed back to the kibbutz across the fields.

As they crossed the olive grove, Morgan's phone buzzed in her pocket. She pulled it out to see Martin's number on the screen.

"Strange that he'd call this early," she said, answering the video call.

His face was haggard, his features drawn, his eyes wide with concern.

"Morgan, I'm so sorry. Your family has been attacked."

CHAPTER 11

Megiddo, Israel.

MORGAN'S HAND FLEW TO her mouth, tears springing to her eyes.

No, please not Faye. Not Gemma.

After her sister and niece had been abducted during the hunt for the Pentecost stones, she had sworn never to endanger their lives again.

"What happened, Martin?" Jake said, taking control as Morgan sank to the ground in shock.

"It's been quite a night, but don't worry, they're safe now."

"Damn it," Morgan exploded with anger, grabbing the phone back. "You scared me, Martin."

"Sorry. I thought you'd want to know straightaway. We installed a special alarm at the Price's house in Woodstock after the Pentecost stones were retrieved. We have something similar in place for the families of all our agents. It was triggered earlier and countermeasures were successfully deployed."

Morgan looked sideways at Jake when she heard the words, but by his raised eyebrows, he clearly didn't know what Martin meant by countermeasures either.

"Several of the intruders were injured," Martin continued, "but Faye and David, and of course, little Gemma, all escaped unharmed. They're staying in the visitor quarters at

ARKANE in Oxford until we can ascertain who attacked."

Morgan remembered her first visit to the labs there, buried deep under the Pitt Rivers section of the Museum of Natural History. It was a fascinating place, and she imagined little Gemma walking wide-eyed through the exhibits at night. But then she thought of her sister Faye, who had survived once before. The sisters didn't speak of any lasting trauma, but it had to be there.

"It looks like we might have disturbed the viper's nest," Jake said. "It has to be Samael and the Brotherhood of the Serpent. They must know of us."

Morgan nodded.

"Are you sure no one can get to my family now, Martin?"

"Of course, we have extra security in place. Don't worry."

She sighed with relief. They were safe for now, but Morgan felt the weight of guilt bear down on her. She considered herself to be independent, beholden to no one except maybe her cat Shmi, back in Oxford, who even preferred the neighbor these days. She and Jake took risks with their own lives for ARKANE, but she had thought her family would be safe. But the night she had seen Faye on top of a pyre, about to be burned as an offering at Pentecost, still haunted her nightmares.

Now her choices had put her family at risk again.

The truth hit Morgan hard. How could she continue at ARKANE when she placed those she loved in danger?

"We've had word from an ARKANE source in the Philippines," Martin continued, breaking into her thoughts. "A deep-sea scientific vessel reported bringing up a large sarcophagus from the depths of the Mariana Trench."

His words cut through Morgan. Could the deepest part of the ocean be the pit described in Revelation? Could the sarcophagus really contain the Great Serpent? The scientist part of her would have laughed at something so crazy not so long ago, but now she wondered.

"If Samael has the sarcophagus," she said, "he will definitely want the seals." She looked out into the darkness. Suddenly her land felt threatening, as looming clouds covered the moon. "We have to get out of here."

"Agreed." Jake stood looking out into the fields around them and Morgan could see that he sensed a heightened danger too. "Where should we go next, Martin?"

"Follow the snake motif through history. You need to head to Greece, to the Pythia."

"The Oracle of Delphi," Morgan whispered. "Of course."

"I'll sort out the flights so you can be on your way as soon as possible." There was a tapping on the line. "I can get you out of Haifa tonight. It's only forty-five minutes' drive."

"Can you get Marietti to give the Tel Megiddo authorities a call?" Jake said. "It might help avoid an incident over taking the seal."

"Sure," Martin said. "Safe travels."

Morgan hung up the phone and sat for a moment, breathing deeply to calm her concerns. Her family was safe inside the ARKANE compound. There was no need to worry about them. She could speak to Faye in the morning, so why did she feel so jumpy?

"Are you OK?" Jake hunkered down next to her, his face a map of concern.

She smiled. "Not really, but we have to get going. I'd like nothing more than to fly back home and cuddle my niece, but we have to finish this. If Samael really has the sarcophagus, we have to hurry."

She stood and they walked back towards the kibbutz together.

"I know you're worried, but aren't you also curious to see what's in that sarcophagus?"

Morgan laughed. As ever, Jake was able to dissipate her fears. "You're right. If it really has been buried for over a thousand years, I want to see inside. It's probably just a pile of dust."

Back at the guest accommodation, they packed their things quickly and left the kibbutz. As time ticked towards dawn, Jake drove them towards Haifa airport in the west while Morgan called Faye on the video phone.

Her sister answered within two rings. Faye's blonde hair was loose about her face and her blue eyes were ringed with dark shadows. The twins had inherited opposite features from their parents, Morgan's dusky features from their Sephardic Jewish father, and Faye's Celtic looks from their Welsh mother. But their eyes were both blue, the unusual slash of violet in Morgan's right eye and in Faye's left the only thing that made them look related.

"Oh, Faye, I'm so sorry. Are you alright? How's Gemma? And David?"

Faye smiled a little. "We're fine. I know you want to be here but none of us are hurt, just a little shaken. David was so paranoid after Pentecost, so Director Marietti at ARKANE helped us install safeguards. I'm sorry we didn't tell you but I didn't want to worry you any more than I know you already do."

"For good reason, clearly." Morgan sighed. "I wish I was there."

"I'll hug Gemma for you. She misses her Auntie M."

"I'll be back soon, I promise. Maybe we can go away for a holiday or something together." Morgan knew she sounded desperate, that she was clinging to an ideal of family life that didn't represent their true relationship. There was so much of the past unsaid and unacknowledged, but Gemma was the real bond between them. A murmur came from beyond the screen and Faye turned her head to mouth something over her shoulder.

"We need to sleep now, Morgan, and we'll be fine here. Gemma loves the ARKANE lab, so it will be like an adventure. Stay safe now."

"OK, sleep tight."

The screen went black and Morgan stared at it for a moment. She was relieved to see her family, but bereft to be so far from them. Not for the first time, she felt a twinge of jealousy at the security of Faye's marriage and the love for her daughter.

Was she fated to run around the world trying to stop bad things happening to people who didn't even notice the darkness around them? Would she spend her life chasing demons, only to die alone in some forgotten corner of an ancient ruin?

Jake put his hand on her arm, glancing over from his focus on the road.

"They're alright?"

Morgan nodded. "Yes, they're fine. Let's finish this so we can go home."

Jake shifted gear and they accelerated into the night towards Haifa airport.

* * *

Grand Canyon Snake Valley Retreat, USA

Lilith loved it down here, curled up on the cool stone of the sarcophagus in the darkness of the sanctuary. Although she had to go upstairs every few hours to bathe in the warmth of the sun and renew her strength, she preferred the chill down here. Layers of deep-sea growth had now dried on the casket, giving it a spongy texture and she lay on top of the softness, still and silent.

Waiting.

Listening.

But as much as she tried, she couldn't hear his voice clearly unless she was in a venom trance. Samael said she must wait and he kept the venom close to him, rationing it, keeping her on edge.

Lilith sighed and dangled one hand over the side of the sarcophagus, touching her fingertips to the indentations. Sam had promised the seals would be delivered in time but she felt an edge of unease, a tension in her spine that could only be released by the opening of the casket.

She longed to see what was inside.

Sam did too, but she sensed his distance now. When she had been just a girl coming out of the church that first night, he had been the one with all the power. He had drawn her, hypnotized her as the serpents within the church had. She had felt languid in his arms.

But now … now he watched her when he thought she wasn't aware. And his gaze was more clinical, as if she were a specimen that he should keep in a case, like his reptiles in the viewing room upstairs.

She heard footsteps on the stair and she froze.

Sam entered the chamber, his gait wary. Lilith slid off the sarcophagus and crouched behind, peering around the end. He narrowed his eyes and squinted in the half-light, unable to see her.

"Lilith?"

She could see him clearly in the dark, but his eyes had not adjusted. For a moment, she saw fear in his expression. Fear of where she might be … Of what she might be.

Lilith smiled, relishing his response. She left him hanging for another few seconds before revealing herself.

"I'm here," she said, straightening.

A look of relief flickered across Sam's face.

"The agents have taken the seal from Megiddo and gone to Delphi in Greece." He frowned. "I know you said to leave them. Was that …" His words trailed off and Lilith knew he didn't want to question the Great Serpent.

"What's wrong?" she asked. "You'll be able to get the seals when they have them all."

"I'm concerned," Sam said. "Krait is excellent and he'll track the agents, but …"

Lilith came closer and pressed her body against Sam's. His heartbeat was fast, a pitter-pat underlined by fear. He didn't belong down here, he was a creature of the mesa and the light.

"But?" she asked.

"I need leverage," Sam said. "The woman's family is now in an ARKANE safe house. Krait's men tried to take them but the attempt failed and now they will be doubly wary." He looked down at Lilith and she sensed that he wanted to be far from her, and far from the sarcophagus. "This is something I need to deal with myself."

"You're going to Europe." Lilith smiled.

"Will you be alright while I'm gone?"

"Will you leave me enough venom?" It was the only thought on her mind.

Sam frowned. "I'll leave enough to keep you going, but we need to save the strongest dose for when we have the seals and can open the casket. Don't take it too far, Lilith." He paused. "I need you."

She could tell it hurt him to admit that. She walked away from him to curl again on top of the sarcophagus. "Don't worry. Just find the seals. He is anxious to emerge and every moment we wait, his anger grows."

* * *

An hour later, Sam boarded the helicopter to take him off the property to Flagstaff airport, then on to Phoenix and London. As they banked over the canyon, he looked down at the lodge as it faded into the mesa, expertly landscaped and camouflaged.

He thought of Lilith down there in the crypt. When he was close to her he was confused, but as the chopper pulled away, he felt like himself again. He shook his head at his previous words.

She was no snake goddess, channeling the Great Serpent.

She was just a junkie he had sought out for her willingness to go into the venom trance, to save his own sanity. But when he found what he sought, when he was finished with her, well, she could have all the venom she wanted.

He texted Krait, determined to regain control. *Get me those seals and finish the agents.*

CHAPTER 12

Delphi, Greece.

THE SUN WAS HIGH as Morgan and Jake reached the town of Delphi and drove up towards the ruins of the ancient sanctuary. After snatching a few hours' sleep on the flight, they had taken turns driving north from Athens and now Morgan turned the car into the carpark. She switched the engine off and got out of the car quickly to stretch.

"Oh, it feels so good to move." She rolled her neck and shoulders, reaching her arms up towards the sun before turning to the view.

Delphi perched on the southwestern slope of Mount Parnassus, surrounded by groves of dusty-green olive trees in a landscape that was similar to the Jezreel Valley they had left just yesterday. It felt timeless, a place of spiritual resonance where seekers journeyed to discover their future.

They headed into the ruins, walking through the ancient classical city along the Sacred Way, the main route through the Sanctuary of Apollo. A group of tourists clustered around the remains of a colonnade, some holding umbrellas to shield them against the Mediterranean sun. Their guide talked into a microphone as he waved his hands with enthusiasm.

"This is the *omphalos*," the guide said. "The very center of the world. It is said that Zeus sent two eagles flying from either ends of the earth and where they crossed, right here, was considered the center."

Jake chuckled a little as they passed by. "Like Rome for Christians," he said under his breath.

"And Jerusalem for Jews." Morgan grinned.

"And Mecca for Muslims. Religion never changes, despite the centuries," Jake said.

"There's a lot of serpent symbolism in various religions too. Ancient Greece had Medusa with her hair of snakes and the Hydra, the nine-headed snake."

Jake put his hands in a prayer position and turned his eyes to heaven. "Please God, don't let us have to battle one of those." He stopped by the ruins of a temple. "But I've got to admit that this place is pretty cool."

The remains of the Temple of Apollo perched on the edge of the hill, with its six Doric columns stretching up into the blue sky. Below them, cypress trees dotted the landscape. Life in the midst of sun-bleached ruins.

"So what happened here, then?" Jake asked.

"There was a shrine, an inner sanctum, where people came to seek the prophecies of the Pythia, the priestess considered the Oracle of Delphi. She sat on a tripod seat over a crack in the earth and the fumes gave her visions of the future. Even kings came to ask the gods for help here."

Morgan understood the desire to ask for guidance from some spiritual force. She felt in need of some herself right now.

In many ways, ARKANE gave her exactly what she needed. A constant stream of fascinating new places, ancient artifacts and puzzles, with an edge of excitement and violence that she now acknowledged as an integral part of herself. She'd tried to shut down that side after leaving the Israeli Defense Force, but it hadn't worked. She'd found academia just too boring to focus on that alone, and her private psychological practice had been repetitive cases with no real challenge.

So why was she now considering leaving ARKANE? And what would she do instead?

"How cool is this, Morgan?"

Jake's voice broke through her thoughts and she turned to see him on a lower level, examining the wall below the temple base.

She smiled at his enthusiasm.

If she stayed at ARKANE, would she and Jake remain just friends, always flirting with the subtle chemistry between them, helping each other stay alive?

If she left, perhaps there would be a chance for them to be together. But then he would always be off doing exciting things, and what would she do? Stay at home and wash dishes?

Like Faye.

Her sister seemed happy being a wife and mother as David performed his duties as the pastor of a church. But as much as Morgan sometimes craved that stable life, she knew she'd probably want to kill something within a week or two.

"Come and see. It's a weird wall," Jake called. Morgan clambered down to see what he was looking at.

The stones that made up the platform were cut into polygonal shapes and carved with ancient inscriptions. One of the stones had the whorl of a snake cut into it, a shape similar to the two other seals she carried in her backpack. But this wasn't a seal. It was just a carving on a stone.

Morgan bent closer. There was something else carved next to it.

"What do you think this is?"

Jake bent to look at it, squinting to try and make sense of the lines. "Maybe a spring? Something to do with water anyway."

"There is a spring here," Morgan said, "where the priestess would ritually wash before entering the temple." She looked at the plan of the ruins and then pointed up to a rocky gorge east of the precinct. "It must be that way."

They walked past the tourists again as they trooped towards the theatre. The semi-circular construction had an incredible view across the valley and Morgan wished they had more time to explore. Instead, they walked onwards towards the Castalian Spring and down a rocky path. Dappled sunlight filtered through the trees. It was a beautiful day, but Morgan felt a prickling on the back of her neck as they reached the bottom. Someone was watching them.

She turned suddenly but there was no one there.

"What is it?" Jake asked, spinning around to look as well.

Morgan frowned. "Maybe nothing, but let's stay alert."

They finally emerged onto a rocky platform that led to the cliff face where two fountains had been cut into the rock within an alcove. A trickle of water came from one.

Jake raised an eyebrow. "That's underwhelming."

Morgan nodded, scanning the area. "This can't be the real place. There's been an ancient spring here since the sixth century BC so this is probably just for the tourists. We need to get to the source, where the origin of power emanated, the most holy place for the serpent." She pointed at a cleft in the rock just around the corner, surrounded by abundant foliage. "That way."

At the edge of the rocky outcrop, they clambered over a low wall and into the dense bushes and trees that hid the cleft in the rock. Jake pushed straight through but Morgan stopped at the edge, turning again as she felt that prickle on the back of her neck.

But once again, there was nobody there.

She frowned and sighed. She usually trusted her instincts, but she knew she was off kilter after the scare with her family. She turned and pushed her way into the trees, finding Jake next to a rocky outcrop.

"Look at this." He stood aside so she could see into the cleft. "It goes a long way back. You think we'll fit?"

"I will." Morgan smiled. "Not sure about you, though."

Jake fake punched her on the arm, sucked his belly in and turned sideways to ease past the rocks. Water dripped down and ferns brushed against Morgan's skin as they twisted up the cleft, eventually reaching the entrance of a cave.

"What *is* that stink?" Jake wrinkled his nose. "It's disgusting."

Morgan bent down to look inside.

"In ancient times," she said, recalling the myth, "the Python was an earth-dragon who made its home here and who became the oracle for Gaia, Mother Earth. But the god Apollo decided he wanted Delphi as his own oracle and killed it. It's said that the priestess, the Pythia, drew her powers from the rotting corpse of the dead snake." She tilted her head to one side and looked up at Jake. "Of course, it could just be bat shit."

Jake snorted with laughter. "Ladies first." He waved towards the entrance with a bow.

Morgan knelt down and opened her pack. She pulled out a head-torch and put it on before crawling into the low tunnel. The stone was wet and it did indeed stink, but within a meter or so, the tunnel expanded out so she could stand. The tinkling of water came from further on. She looked up and the light from her head-torch caught the whorls and loops of a gigantic snake carved on the ceiling. She turned and called back to Jake.

"Get in here and look at this."

Moments later, he crawled in with his own head-torch on and looked up.

"Oh yeah, that's a snake alright."

"And its head points further in."

Morgan felt a rising excitement, a sense that this place was the true sacred spot on the mountain, not the manmade columns of the temples outside. This place was closer to the Gaia, Mother Earth, and closer to her creatures. Closer to life … and death.

She shone her head-torch in the direction of the snake's head and at the back of the cave, there was another hole. They walked over to it.

"This is quite a bit narrower than the entrance." Jake frowned as he shone his light through. "But it's quite short."

"Do you want to stay here while I go on?"

"No way. Where you go, I go." Jake grinned. "Most of the time anyway."

Morgan pushed the backpack ahead of her through the hole and wiggled in. She stretched her hands out in front and pulled herself along while using her feet to push. She tried not to think about the tons of rock above her.

Once in the next chamber, she helped pull Jake through and he collapsed on the floor.

"A little too tight for my liking," he said, after regaining his breath. "It better not get any narrower." Then he looked up and his torchlight played on the walls. "But maybe we don't have to go any further."

Morgan turned to look.

The entire chamber was decorated with carvings, the rock hewn with images of nature. Deer leapt over fish swimming in streams, while birds flew overhead. A cornucopia of nature's bounty. The colors had faded with time but clearly there had been worshippers here more recently. A wilted bunch of wildflowers sat on the edge of a spring. It was just rough-hewn rock with edges discolored by minerals that flowed from within the mountain. But something about it made Morgan's breath catch in her throat. The sound of tinkling water resounded in the cave, a constant hymn to the Creator.

Behind the glistening water, Morgan caught sight of a circular object.

"There, behind the spring."

Jake diverted the flow with his hands, the fresh water splashing over his shoes while Morgan took a closer look.

"It's the seal," she said. "It's a similar size to the others, but the snake is curled in a slightly different way."

"Can you lever it out?"

Morgan pulled a multi-tool from her pack and began to lever the rock from the spring. How long had it been here? Who had put the seals in places sacred to serpents around the world? Part of her wanted to study the stone carvings, to try and work out what their power was. She was fascinated by how old they could be. But part of her wanted to find a way to crush the stones into powder as fast as possible, ending their mission so she could go back home.

The stone popped free and Jake let the spring run in its natural place again. He cupped some of the water and brought it to his mouth.

"Tastes good," he said. "Despite the smell."

Morgan took a sip. Perhaps the Pythia of ancient Greece had drunk from this spring long ago. She smiled to herself at the romantic thought.

"Let's get out of here," she said, after a moment.

Jake eyed the tunnel and Morgan caught the look on his face.

"I'll go first and help you through again, you big baby."

She pushed the backpack in again and crawled after it. Jake huffed behind her, his breathing shallow as he tried to make his substantial size much smaller. She emerged into the cave tunnel.

"I need a hand," Jake called from back inside, his light flickering around her.

Morgan placed the backpack with the seals on the cave floor, needing both hands to help him through. She squeezed halfway back into the tunnel and reached for him.

"Grab my hands and I'll pull while you twist."

As she tugged, Jake wriggled and by inches, he made his way through the tiny space.

Then a noise came from behind her in the cave.

Morgan couldn't see, couldn't turn around quickly. Her startled eyes met Jake's.

"Go, I can make the last few inches," he said.

Morgan shuffled backwards into the cave and turned her light to the floor.

The backpack was gone.

With all three seals inside.

The sound of running footsteps came from the tunnel that headed towards the entrance. She sprinted towards the noise, her light bobbing through the cave. Behind her, she heard Jake swearing and a thud as he pulled himself out of the tunnel. Then he joined in the chase.

Morgan turned a corner and saw a man silhouetted at the low entrance.

He ducked under.

She heard a click and then a series of popping noises. She knew the sound from her time in the Israeli Defense Force. She threw herself back and down on the floor.

"Down, Jake!" she shouted, as the cave exploded around her.

CHAPTER 13

A s   t h e   d u s t   f r o m   the explosion settled, Krait emerged from the cypress tree he had sheltered behind. He crouched down and checked the backpack for the three seals and smiled as he examined each in turn.

Samael would be pleased.

He glanced back at the now-buried entrance to the cave. There was no way of checking whether the agents inside were still alive but they should at least be trapped and injured, hopefully dead. Whatever state they were in, they were delayed and he had the seals. But the noise of the explosion would bring rescuers soon enough, so he needed to get away from here.

Krait texted Samael. *I have them. Where shall I meet you?*

He walked back down the rocky path towards the carpark where site officials busied themselves for a rescue operation. Tourists bustled around taking pictures of the drama, confusing the scene. Krait walked into a pack of them, a concerned look on his face, well-hidden amongst the many nationalities represented. Using their cover, he made his way back to the car. As he drove out the carpark, joining the throng heading away from the mountain, his phone beeped with an incoming message.

Excellent. Come to London.

* * *

Inside the cave, Morgan stirred. She felt a sense of crushing weight upon her as she woke from the blackness. Her head pounded and she tried to lift her left arm.

There was something on it. She couldn't move.

Pins and needles prickled her flesh. A trapped nerve. Not good.

Her right hand was free, though, and she lifted it to her face, gingerly touching her temple where the pain was greatest. Her fingers met sticky wetness and she probed a dripping wound. She winced as she tested the edges but it felt shallow, nothing serious. Her whole body ached but after years in the military and plenty of injuries with ARKANE, she understood her own pain levels. She would be alright – if they got out of here soon.

But what the hell had happened?

Morgan opened her eyes. It was pitch black. The air smelled of tar under the sickening stench of the rotten python, or whatever the hell that smell was. The bastard who stole the packs must have set off an explosion as he left.

"Jake?" she whispered in the dark. "Are you OK?"

A deep groan came from her left.

Then she felt a hand reach out for her. She gripped it and for a moment, they just lay there in the dark, the physical connection all they needed. Morgan took some deep breaths, letting calm wash over her. They were alive. They were together.

"He took the backpack," she said eventually, as she began to feel a little better.

"Of course he did," Jake growled. "But he could have just stolen it. Why the hell did he have to blow us up?" The sound of rocks shifting echoed in the cave. "At least you didn't make it to the entrance, though. Another twenty meters closer and you'd be buried."

Morgan heard the concern in his voice. She remembered the explosion they'd been in at the Palermo Capuchin crypt and how his injuries that night had filled her with the same worry. At least they weren't surrounded by broken bits of mummified bodies in here.

"I can't move my arm," she said. "Any chance you can help?"

"Just a sec." A tiny light flared and then grew in warmth. Morgan saw Jake's face in the light of the yellow glow-stick. "Good job I still have my pack." Jake grinned and Morgan couldn't help but smile back, despite the pain in her arm and her head. There was something primeval in having light in the darkness. It made everything instantly better.

He clambered over the fallen rocks towards her. "Right, let's get you out of there."

* * *

It was another four hours before they heard the clunk of stones being removed and the shouts of voices beyond the cave-in. Morgan had fallen asleep, cradled in Jake's arms, but woke again as he moved at the sound. The pounding in her head made her nauseous and her arm throbbed. Thoughts of her family rose in her mind. Faye strapped to a pyre. Gemma unconscious in the arms of a madman. She knew they were safe, but she longed to be with them.

"Stay there," Jake said, gently stroking her face as he helped her sit back against the cave wall. He rose and went to the pile of broken stone.

"We're in here!" he called through the cracks.

A triumphant shout came back, the words unintelligible, but soon they saw torchlight as the rocks at the side of the tunnel were pulled away.

Jake joined in, hefting stones until he could touch the hand of one of the rescuers beyond.

"Hang in there," the man said. "Here, I'm passing through provisions." He pushed through a parcel and a flask. "We'll have you out soon. Is anyone injured?"

"My friend's arm was crushed in the fall and she might have concussion from a minor head injury."

The rescuer nodded. "We'll hurry."

Jake took the food and drink over to Morgan, pouring hot coffee from the flask and handing it to her. "Here, drink this." He helped her to sip the bitter black and Morgan felt a wave of relief sweep over her. Coffee always helped.

They devoured the sweet pastries together and the sugar buoyed them both as they waited for the tunnel to be widened further.

The rescuers broke through soon after. A medic tended to Morgan's arm, before they scrambled from the cave out into the late-afternoon sun.

* * *

A little while later, Morgan sat in the back of an ambulance. Her arm was patched up and in a temporary sling. Her head was bandaged, and with a full dose of painkillers, plus sugar and caffeine, she was feeling comparatively better. Jake was on the phone to Marietti.

"Yes, the seals are gone but we're just about OK. I think we can travel." He looked over at Morgan and she smiled back, nodding her head that yes, she was alright. "Where do you want us to go next?" He paused. "Right. Later then."

He hung up and turned to her. "Marietti wants us back in London. There are too many options for where to go next. And he wanted me to tell you that your family are still safe."

Morgan looked out at the setting sun over the valley. It was beautiful, a timeless place where so many had come to seek the will of the gods. The smell of olive trees and warm earth lingered on the air. "Let's not rush back."

CHAPTER 14

ARKANE Headquarters, London.

MARTIN KLEIN WALKED AROUND his desk to the wall of his office and examined the colored markers arrayed in a rainbow from light to dark. This called for crimson and cerulean blue. He picked up the particular pens and began to draw directly on the office walls, allowing the critical part of his mind to relax as he shaded and cross-hatched and spiraled across the white.

Despite his many technological tools, Martin had learned that his mind sometimes just figured things out this way. While some people had ideas in the shower, he found inspiration in drawing. It distracted his analytical mind and enabled him to find the most peculiar connections. Of course, his office had to be repainted every few months, or whenever he had solved whatever problem was most pressing. A small price to pay for clarity.

Most of Martin's time was spent immersed in computer code as part of his role as ARKANE's archivist, although he was basically a hacker on behalf of the agency. He had yet to come up against a system he could not get into. His main concern was the knowledge locked away in physical texts and symbolic objects, that which was *not* digitalized.

And that's what haunted him now. Because something was very wrong indeed.

The hunt for the seals was just one aspect, but there were too many other things happening at the same time. The news reported developments daily, an increase in violence done in the name of religion, a sudden influx of natural disasters and death caused by extreme weather, earthquakes and rising oceans.

And then there was the series of blood moons, which drove the fundamentalists crazy as they claimed that biblical prophecies were coming true.

So it had to be one of two things.

Either it really was the End Times, the final days of Earth as humanity knew it and the imminent beginning of a new order ushered in by celestial trumpets and great destruction by the Almighty …

Or, someone was pulling the strings from behind the scenes, engineering a growing crisis that could spill over into something unstoppable. God helps those who help themselves, after all. World War Three would not be sparked by one event, but tensions were mounting. All it took was one significant flashpoint to trigger the end.

Something itched at the back of Martin's mind, and he had grown to trust that feeling. When he had first joined ARKANE, Jake had fondly nicknamed him Spooky for his uncanny ability to find connections in the mass of data and knowledge. Martin was proud of the title and wanted to remain deserving of it. There were few people he valued in the world, and Jake was one of them. Perhaps he would even count him as a friend, although the rules of such a relationship puzzled Martin a little.

He understood his own condition. He'd spent time researching why his parents had been so disappointed with him despite his incredible academic achievements. A PhD from Cambridge by seventeen years old, and yet they just wanted him to get a girlfriend. Asperger's would have been a handicap in any other era but in this technological age, it was a true gift.

Martin understood the world of numbers and code and logic, but he couldn't understand why people behaved the way they did, and why they didn't say what they really meant. ARKANE had been a haven and Director Marietti had taken him in, allowing him to push the boundaries of his gift, accepting him for who he was with no pressure to conform to any societal norm. But then ARKANE was a haven for all kinds of misfits. It suited those who wanted an extraordinary life, not those whose idea of fun was watching Netflix on a Friday night with a pizza and a bottle of wine.

Jake had been friendly from the start, and Morgan … Martin smiled at the thought of her. Morgan seemed to truly understand him. Perhaps there was a touch of his own dysfunction in her fierce independence.

Marietti, Jake and Morgan were his true family and he sensed they were in danger now. He had to figure out what the hell was going on and for once, his computer couldn't help him. All the hacking in the world couldn't find something that wasn't codified in bits and bytes.

He stopped drawing and ran his fingers through his hair, tugging at the roots. Some of the strands came out in his fingers and he brushed them to the floor. It was a bad habit, but pulling his hair out actually helped him think, and he certainly wasn't bothered by what people thought of his appearance.

So far, the picture on the wall undulated with the coils of a massive serpent. He began to draw the various clues they had found around it, and then expanded it into the signs that had appeared in the world. The freak weather events, high tides and super storms that rocked every continent. The sarcophagus found in the deepest ocean, thought by some to be the resting place of the Great Serpent.

But that wasn't all.

In the last weeks, Director Marietti had been targeted by those who wished to stop him investigating the Babylonian prophecy of the serpent. Because they knew he would send Morgan and Jake to find out more. They knew he would try to stop whatever had been set in motion. The bomb that had blown open the vault was directed with deadly accuracy and only someone on the inside would know the vault's exact location.

What if the whole India mission had been planned to keep ARKANE occupied while the End Times progressed towards its inevitable conclusion? If Marietti had been killed, ARKANE London would have been crippled. So, who had known about all of this?

Something pricked at the corners of his mind.

Martin went back to his computer and checked the inventory of the vault, recently updated after the damage from the bombing. Amongst the priceless objects and artifacts of supernatural power, there were also records from the earliest days of ARKANE that he had discovered in the aftermath of the explosion. The original annals, the founding documents. Records that were so old they had to be read in a climate-controlled atmosphere.

Records he had yet to digitize.

Martin scurried from his office and headed down to the lower levels in one of the lifts. The whole area had been reinforced with extra security, so he scanned his retina and then typed in a passcode to get the lift moving.

At the basement level, the door opened onto a corridor reinforced overhead. It wouldn't stop a bunker-busting bomb, but it would prevent pretty much anything else getting through.

Martin walked to the thick metal door overlaid with ancient wood. It was inscribed with occult patterns that once upon a time might have made someone think twice about entering. But now the door was criss-crossed with modern steel bars and protected by a high-level electronic security system updated after the last attack and protected with a steel cage. Martin typed in another code and then placed his finger on a pad. It was sensitized to certain individuals within ARKANE; if their heartbeat was too fast and fell outside the normal range, the system went into security lockdown.

Martin calmed his breathing. The door clicked open.

He stepped inside the vault and breathed in the rarefied air as he walked past individual rooms containing treasures that the world thought lost to history. Part of ARKANE's job was to recover powerful artifacts and hide them here, away from the clutches of those who might use them for evil. Morgan and Jake had placed the Pentecost stones here, the Devil's Bible, the staff of Skara Brae and other objects that needed protection.

Or that the world needed protection from.

But there were also records of ARKANE, the annals of its birth and growth, lists of Directors and the agents who had given their lives for the secrets down here and yet could never be acknowledged in public. Martin hoped that the Director would never have to inscribe Jake or Morgan's name in these books.

He walked to the back of the vault to a special area filled with towering shelves loaded with great leather-bound books. He found the right date range and then used the wheeled ladder to climb a meter up. He ran his finger along the cracked spines until he located the book he wanted and then pulled it down. The dates 1880–1900 were etched in gold on the spine.

The escalating news cycle from Israel had been bothering Martin the most, as biblical prophecies stated over and over again that the Jews must be back in their ancient homeland for the End Time events to occur.

It could be argued that the Chosen People had been protected over the many generations they had been persecuted, broken apart and spread across the world in a diaspora that spanned the globe. But despite oppression by Egypt, Assyria, Babylon, Persia, Greece and Rome in ancient times, and from much anti-Semitism, pogroms, death camps and more in modern times, the Jewish people had survived. Perhaps God really did have a hand in their survival, but Martin had his suspicions that there was more to it.

He found the page he wanted, an account from 1897, when ARKANE representatives had been at the first Zionist Congress supporting Theodor Herzl in the goal of reclaiming the land of Israel. He looked at the names, recognizing the title of a Cardinal from the Vatican. Not unusual by itself.

But then Martin found something curious.

Minutes from a meeting between the same Cardinal and the Mufti of Jerusalem, a Muslim. There was nothing concrete, only veiled references to a long-buried cistern and a joint project that would safeguard the future of both religions even as Israel expanded.

Martin narrowed his eyes. There must be more.

He climbed the stairs again and pulled down more books, pushing them to the floor with a series of crashes. He clambered down and sat cross-legged, pulling each one onto his lap as he scanned for more such meetings.

A note from the Imam of Iran thanking the ARKANE Vatican liaison for support. A receipt for services rendered during the Gulf War. A picture of a multi-faith group of men in front of the statue of Laocoon, with the priest and his sons dying in the grip of writhing serpents.

The more he read, the more Martin realized that the Vatican and ARKANE seemed to be part of a bigger plan that also involved fundamentalists on both the Jewish and the Muslim sides.

They were sworn enemies, but they also desired a new world order, albeit of a different shade. All wanted to hasten the apocalypse. What if the mortal enemies engineered a world-ending battle together?

Could anyone stop that?

Until the thousand years were ended. The words spoken by Cardinal Krotalia echoed around his head. He needed to get this to Marietti.

Suddenly there was a clunk and a click. The lights went out in the vault.

Martin spun around, his hands still on the book. The vault door was closed. A hissing came from nozzles above. He had installed the upgrades to the security himself.

A poisonous gas would flood the vault in the next three minutes.

CHAPTER 15

ARKANE vault, London.

MARTIN SCRAMBLED TO HIS feet and ran towards the door, slipping on the polished floor in his haste.

"Stop. I'm still in here!" he shouted, hoping it was a mistake. Maybe Marietti had come down for something. He reached the massive door and pounded upon it with his fists, but no sound came from outside. Whoever had shut him in was gone.

The hissing sound grew stronger as the gas escaped from the nozzles above.

He coughed and covered his mouth, bending lower to the ground to keep his face away. If he succumbed before he could get out, then the ARKANE vault would be his final resting place. As much as he loved it here, that wasn't how he intended to go.

Jake had told him once of a rumored escape route from the vault, something placed here just in case. Like so much of ARKANE, there was always another way. Nothing was left to chance.

But where was it?

Martin wracked his brain trying to remember the off-hand conversation. He hadn't paid much attention at the time, but it was something about a curse of kings channeled through a woman of heaven …

He stumbled to one of the side vaults marked with symbols of ancient Egypt, noticing anew the stylized uraeus cobra on the crown of the pharaohs. The serpent was everywhere and he cursed it now. Dizzy, Martin sank to the floor. He crawled into the vault, willing himself to go on. Jake wouldn't give up, and thoughts of his friend spurred him on.

The space was filled with boxes covered in stamps and labels, each one containing something precious and powerful. But none of those could help him now. Martin's eyes fixed on the standing sarcophagus against the back wall. The anthropoid inner coffin of Seshepenmehyt, carved from sycamore fig and dated to around 600 BC.

He dragged himself to the coffin and looked up. The face of the long-dead noblewoman painted in dark green stared down at him. Under the decorated collar, the goddess Nut spread her wings, goddess of the sky and the heavens.

Doubt flooded Martin's mind but as the opaque gas began to fill the room, he knew it was his only chance. He pulled himself up, desperately feeling for any way to open the sarcophagus. His fingers found a notch in the side and he pressed it. The door swung open.

He gasped in horror.

The mummy stood wrapped in bandages, brown with the patina of age. He imagined scarab beetles crawling through the layers, eating the dead flesh inside.

But then his logical mind kicked in.

There was no way a real Egyptian mummy would be kept in the ARKANE vault, even with its special climate control. It must be a fake.

He grimaced with disgust but steeled himself to reach out and pull the mummy from the case. It crashed down to the floor and he pushed it away with his foot, the spongy corpse making him shiver. The hiss of gas increased its frequency and Martin began to feel faint again. He clambered into the sarcophagus and pulled the door shut with a click, trapping himself in darkness. He could sense the boundaries of the tiny space, the wood only inches from his nose. It smelled of incense and the sweet, cloying scent of death. His breathing grew shallow and he panted and coughed, wheezing with pain.

He had made a terrible mistake.

With a horrible dread, he felt for a catch on the inside of the sarcophagus, his fingers desperately scrabbling for something that would get him out of here again. Was he trapped? Would he die here in the vault?

Martin tried to channel Jake's confidence. What would his friend do? If this was really the emergency way out, it wouldn't be obvious. The mummy was a decoy, of that he was sure, so there must be something else here. He pressed himself back against the rear wall, his fingers sweeping the wood from side to side as he shuffled up and down, desperation rising in his chest.

Suddenly, he felt a groove in the wood.

Martin pressed a finger inside and heard a faint click. Relief flooded through him and he let out the breath he hadn't realized he had been holding. The lower half of the mummy case behind him dropped away, creating enough space for him to back out and crawl into a thin, low tunnel. Emergency lighting in the floor meant that he could see a little way into the darkness. The shadows threw an eerie light before him.

He bent over to walk down the low tunnel, scurrying away from the vault. He didn't know who had locked him in, but he couldn't go back to the ARKANE office now. He needed to get to Jake and Morgan. They would know what to do.

* * *

Delphi, Greece.

Morgan sat on the edge of the pool at the Delphi Palace Hotel. Her legs dangled in cool water as the sound of cicadas filled the balmy air. It smelled of lemon thyme and the coconut of spilled suntan lotion and she smiled, enjoying a moment of normality in the craziness of an ARKANE mission. Right now, there was nothing else to do but wait.

Jake walked out of the hotel room carrying two glasses, ice chinking against the side as he sat down next to her.

"Gin and tonic," he said. "Local gin but hey, it's better than nothing."

Morgan took the drink. "Cheers."

They touched glasses, eyes meeting in the semi-darkness. As ever, there was too much to say but Morgan understood Jake's relief at her recovery. She hadn't enjoyed seeing him in hospital, but thankfully this time, they had both escaped severe injury.

She took a sip, letting the aromatics fill her senses. She sighed. "That is so good."

They sat for a moment in silence, savoring the night air. Jake's leg brushed against hers in the water and Morgan entwined her ankle around his.

He turned to her. "Morgan, I–"

His phone buzzed in his pocket. The moment was broken. Jake pulled it out and answered.

"Martin, what's up?" His face paled and he stood up on the water's edge. "It's OK. Calm down. Here's what you need to do."

Jake paced up and down by the side of the pool as he explained an escape plan from London. When he finally hung up, his face was serious.

"Martin was almost killed in the ARKANE vault. Someone shut him in there."

Morgan frowned. "Someone on the inside."

"Exactly. I've sent him to one of my emergency drops so he'll be able to make it out."

Morgan raised an eyebrow. "Emergency drop?"

Jake hunkered down next to her, his face inches from hers, his eyes amused. "Oh, I expect you have several, Ms Sierra." He smiled, his corkscrew scar twisting with humor. "Perhaps I'll get to see them one day."

Morgan laughed. It was good to be here with Jake, just a pair of secret agents now apparently on the run. "Is Martin coming here?"

Jake walked back towards the hotel room. "Sorry, but we're going to have to break up the party. He saw something in the archives that he thinks might be important, so we're going to meet him in Rome."

* * *

Vatican City, Rome, Italy.

"This is terrible coffee." Jake grimaced as he gulped the black liquid down.

Morgan gestured at the grand entrance to the Vatican Museums in front of them. "But look at the view." She checked her watch. "Martin should be here by now. I hope he's alright."

"I supervised his mandatory field training. He'll be fine." Jake took a bite of his flaky cornetto pastry.

They had driven back to Athens and flown out on the last night flight to Rome. Jake had stayed in touch with Marietti, but neither had mentioned Martin's escape. ARKANE was clearly compromised and the Director would find out something was up soon enough. In the meantime, they would try to get ahead of whoever was trying to sabotage the mission.

Morgan's head had been pounding by the time they

landed and found a hotel. Jake had insisted on sleeping on the couch in her room, worried about concussion. She had watched him in the dark, wanting him to hold her but saying nothing. She had slept soon after and woke in the morning light to find him sorting out tickets to the Vatican Museum. They had arranged to meet Martin in the closest cafe to the entrance, hence the bad coffee. Still, any coffee was better than no coffee at this point.

She looked across the road to the entrance, the marble door carved with the words Musei Vaticani. It was flanked either side by a towering wall and tourists snaked in a line away down the hill. Morgan knew from bitter experience that the queue could go on for several kilometers, which is why they had sorted tickets in advance using ARKANE connections.

Just then, Morgan saw a tall man with a shock of messy blonde hair scurrying up the hill towards them.

"Un altro caffè, per favore." She gestured to the waiter and he brought another espresso just as Martin reached their table. There were deep shadows under his eyes, barely concealed by his wire-rim glasses and he rubbed his hands together in an anxious, repetitive movement.

Jake pulled a chair out for him. "Sit down, Spooky. Take a breath. We can't go in yet. They haven't opened the gates."

Martin sat down with a pained expression. Morgan could see he was disturbed by his flight from the ARKANE offices. She didn't know where he called home, but he spent so much time under Trafalgar Square that it was likely he had a bed there. She knew what exile felt like, and she wanted to reach out a hand to comfort him. But Martin wasn't one for physical contact, so she just pushed the espresso over to him. He gave a half smile and a long exhalation, then leaned across the table towards them.

"I'm worried about going in there," he whispered. "I found things in the vault that suggest the Vatican is involved in this End Times conspiracy. Perhaps one of their own shut me in the vault."

Jake snorted with laughter. "Of course they're involved. That's not news. The Church has a vested interest in keeping people believing in the End Times. No doubt the fundamentalists within want to usher in that day of reckoning."

Morgan nodded. "Jake has a point there. The question is whether this is a move towards something more concrete."

Martin pulled out his smart phone. "I think this goes beyond eschatology in the academic sense." He swiped to find a picture and turned it to show them. "This is an interfaith meeting. This man is Jewish, this one Muslim and these are Cardinals. Look where they're standing."

Morgan took the phone and zoomed in. "That's the statue of Laocoon. That's why we're here." As she spoke, the massive gates opened in front of them and early-bird tourists began to file into the museum complex. "Let's go see what we can find."

"And try to get out again before anyone knows we're here," Martin said.

Together, they walked into the Museum. Morgan wished they had more time because it didn't matter how many times she visited, there was always more to see here. The Vatican Museums were a treasure trove of history, a place to delve into the magnificence of what humans could create in the name of God. The Jewish tradition she came from wasn't big on over-decoration but she appreciated the extravagant beauty of the Vatican, even though the current Pope deplored the wealth of the Church and wished to give it all away to the poor. Perhaps those who opposed his reforms were part of this End Times plan.

They walked on through the corridors, heading for the Museo Pio-Clementino, one of the sculpture museums surrounding the Cortile del Belvedere. They passed the porphyri sarcophagi of Constance and Saint Helen, a gilded bronze of Hercules, the sleeping Ariadne and a grouping of Apollo and the Muses. Morgan was grateful for the acceptance of these pagan images within the hallowed walls of the Vatican. After all, it was these classical statues that inspired Michelangelo to paint the figures on the ceiling of the Sistine Chapel, the glorious male nudes that were the models for Adam and God himself.

They finally reached the courtyard where the Laocoon statue stood in a niche. Morgan walked around it slowly. Despite the number of significant classical figures within the museum, this one stood out in its portrayal of human agony. The marble sculpture immortalized the perfection of the male nude, outlining each straining muscle of the tortured priest. The classical themes of suffering and death pervaded the Vatican, but this statue was pagan, depicting a death that did not end in redemption. Thankfully the Christians of the modern era were not so threatened by these ancient gods that they had destroyed all mention of them.

Morgan bent closer to examine how the fangs of one snake sank into the priest's thigh, just as an official Vatican guide walked up, leading a group of tourists. A few keen photographers crowded near the front and the usual bored teenagers trailed behind their parents, tapping away on their screens. Morgan wondered briefly if Pokémon Go had made it into the Vatican. Perhaps it would rejuvenate the interest of the young if they made it part of the experience.

"Laocoon was a Trojan priest of Poseidon who tried to stop the Trojan horse destroying the city by revealing what was inside." The guide's delivery was clipped, a practiced speech. "But the Gods had their own plans and he was punished for his attempt to disrupt the path of Fate. Poseidon sent sea serpents to devour the priest and his sons for daring to meddle with the divine plan."

She took a breath before continuing. "The style of the sculpture is known as Pergamene baroque from Greece and

Asia Minor around two hundred years before Christ. The most famous example is demonstrated on the Pergamon Altar, reconstructed in the museum named after it in Berlin."

Morgan started at the mention of the Pergamon Museum and her eyes darted to Jake's. He looked as surprised as she did by the revelation. Could this be the link they were looking for?

CHAPTER 16

Jerusalem, Israel.

THE ENTRANCE TO THE vault was hidden at the back of a guesthouse run by the silent Sisters of Charity. It was used only by select members of the Vatican, those who were part of the greater plan, whose theology leaned towards the eschatological. Cardinal Eric Krotalia glanced at his watch as he stalked through the house. He was going to be a few minutes late after a hold-up at the airport and then the rigmarole of trying to lose any potential tail in the warren of the Old City.

But the precautions were important at this stage. They were so close now.

He hurried to one of the cupboards and pulled out a suitcase. He couldn't proceed without changing and removing all traces of his true identity. He took out the hooded robe of plain hessian and put it over his casual jeans and t-shirt attire, not what most would expect from a Cardinal in Jerusalem. His running shoes peeked out from below the robe, necessary for the unstable stairs and walk ahead. Despite his sixty-five years, the Cardinal felt fitter than ever.

More than ready for the times to come.

He paused as he reached for the snakeskin belt. He ran a finger along its length, reveling in the texture of raised scales. It was brilliant blue with a red stripe along the length, skin from a California red-sided garter snake, caught within a few miles of his own home in Monterey County. According to the ancient tradition of the Brotherhood, he had caught, skinned and treated it himself. He stroked the snakeskin and smiled with pride as he picked it up and tied it around his waist. It was thinner than the scarlet fascia he wore as part of his official choir dress, and he liked how the two were a line between his alternate worlds. One must walk in the darkness to fully appreciate the light. And to usher in the End Times was a crucial role indeed.

He took off his Cardinal's ecclesiastical ring and laid it by the bedside. As the final step, he picked up the matching snakeskin mask that would obscure the top half of his face, turning his eyes into serpent-like slits so as to protect his identity. He would put that on downstairs, just in case he surprised one of the nuns.

It was time to go.

He walked back downstairs and out towards a plain wooden door in the kitchen. It looked just like a pantry but behind it, stairs had been cut into the rock that wound down and under the city. They led to an ancient cistern, one of thirty mapped by Sir Charles Wilson in 1864, back when the Temple Mount was not such a flashpoint for religious extremism. It was forbidden to go down in the cisterns now.

At least officially.

But the old maps had been useful to locate this particular cistern, and it served the Brotherhood's purpose well. The houses were closely packed here in the Old City and this corner of the Jewish Quarter backed almost directly onto the Temple Mount, one of the holiest Islamic shrines and controlled by Muslim authorities. Armed guards walked the perimeter, automatic weapons at the ready. At the same time, Israeli soldiers patrolled the site of the Western Wall, both sides preventing extremists from either religion from doing anything that might disturb the fragile knife-edge of peace in this city.

But the time was coming when the commonalities of the great religions would matter far more than the differences.

The tunnel had taken many years to form, the rock dissolved by special acids and then chiseled away so as to be almost silently constructed. The price for being discovered would be instantaneous and catastrophic but so far they had avoided detection. The status quo of the Holy Land site remained untouched, put in place by the Ottoman Sultan in 1757 to protect freedom of worship. The Cardinal knew that the Christian emperors and kings would never have allowed such a ruling, but the current Israeli administration enforced respect for the status quo and as such, the Temple Mount was under the protection of the King of Jordan.

But the status quo would not stand for much longer.

The Cardinal opened the door and clicked on the lights inside. Dim bulbs hung on metal brackets illuminating stone steps, a dull yellow light casting a sulfur glow. Water dripped down the walls and he walked slowly down, holding onto the lumps in the stone to prevent himself from slipping in the wet patches.

He wiped a bead of sweat from his brow as he descended. There was so little time left and much more to do. He worried more about discovery after what had happened at ARKANE. After Marietti had somehow gotten hold of that tablet, he had tried to direct their agents away from the truth. But now their archivist had escaped his trap and would be investigating further. He couldn't be seen around there anymore. It was imperative that Samael focused on retrieving the seals.

The air smelled musty, like an animal lair where half-digested carcasses lay in the corners. He had tried to direct fresh air into the cistern below, but it still held the scent of death and decay. Perhaps that was only natural. After all, this particular spot in Jerusalem had been the site of thousands of years of conflict, of blood spilled on all sides. It was only right that it absorb the scent of death. And there was much more blood to come, if their plans proceeded on track.

The Cardinal finally reached the bottom and hurried as much as he could down the tunnel. He didn't like to be late. There was enough jostling for position in the Brotherhood as it was and he didn't like to leave the others alone for too long.

Raised voices echoed in the tunnel and his pulse raced at the thought of the sound filtering up to the Temple Mount above. Sometimes he wondered whether his trust in them was even justified. The other two had their own entrances and he didn't even know where they emerged, so secret were the details of their construction. Each understood the consequences of discovery, but tensions were rising between them.

He put his mask on as he turned the final corner and pulled up the hood of his tunic to cover his head as he entered the main chamber. The cistern had been used in the time of the First Temple, later buried by the double destruction of the city above. It lay directly under the Dome of the Rock and to the east of the Western Wall, a secret compartment only meters from two of the most contested sacred sites in the world.

The Cardinal stood silently for a moment as the other two men turned at his entrance.

"Brothers, be calm," he said quietly. "We're so close now. What could be more important than ushering in the climactic battle between Good and Evil at the apotheosis of history? We must work together in these final days."

The two men fell silent and shuffled to the center of the chamber to meet him.

The Cardinal glanced around. The three of them were the highest ranking of the Roshites, the Brotherhood of the Serpent. Each wore a snake around his waist and covered his face. Although they were meant to be anonymous, the Cardinal knew enough about each man. As they likely knew the truth of his own double life within the Vatican. But together, they had a more important mission.

The End of Days.

"It is true. Our differences are nothing." The man known as Cerastes wore a desert horned viper and spoke with an Iraqi accent. He was bent with age but his grip was still iron hard. He controlled a vast army of devotees under the auspices of what some called freedom fighters, and others called terrorists. Cerastes believed he was living in the era of the return of the Mahdi, a messianic figure prophesied in the *hadith*, a collection of the Prophet's deeds and sayings.

Some days, the Cardinal was jealous of Cerastes. It was easy for him to incite his followers to violence and decisive action, whereas the American congregations he was responsible for were much happier giving money than their lives to the cause.

But that would change soon enough because there would be something to unite against.

"What news, brother?" The third man, Echis, was tall and lithe and moved like a soldier with barely restrained violence. He wore a saw-scaled viper, the dark and lighter brown stripes tied almost double around his waist, evidence of how big the creature had been in life. The Cardinal imagined Echis crushing it with those meaty hands in the desert sand, his dark eyes showing no compassion as he broke its skull. Echis was an extremist Jew and a Zionist, the final side to their triangle.

Between the three of them, they represented the great monotheistic religions, the faiths that believed in an end time and together they would usher it in.

Each believed the others to be wrong about the details of the coming apocalypse, but they had enough in common to begin the countdown together. God would know his own once the slaughter began.

"There have been a few setbacks." The Cardinal dipped his head in a slight apology.

Cerastes coughed, a wet sound that echoed in the chamber. "Where is the sarcophagus?"

"In a safe place."

"In America, you mean."

The Cardinal nodded. "But it will be transferred in the next few days. The details for shipping are being finalized. It will travel with objects for an exhibition at Hebrew University. Don't worry. It will be here in time for the alignment."

Echis nodded. "I can confirm the transit details and will ensure the sarcophagus is brought here as soon as it arrives."

The Cardinal took a deep breath. "There is a woman who will travel with it. Samael believes she can hear the Great Serpent speak, that she channels His thoughts."

Echis grunted. "You believe this?"

The Cardinal hesitated, thinking of what Samael had told him about Lilith. Then he nodded. "The risks are too great to lose one of us to the other side of the venom trance. She is a conduit until He is risen."

"And when we bring her here?" Cerastes grunted.

The Cardinal nodded. "She will be the first sacrifice to the Great Serpent, as it has been foretold."

"There has always been a woman in the prophecy," Cerastes said. "But what about the seals? The alignment is only days away."

"We have four of them. There are still three more to find." There was a heavy sense of disappointment in the room and the Cardinal felt it was all directed at him. It was time to change tack.

"What of the preparations for the battle at Dabiq?" the Cardinal asked Cerastes pointedly.

The city in Syria was mentioned in a *hadith* describing events of the *Malahim*, roughly translated as Armageddon. It was meant to be the site of one of the End Times battles between Muslims and modern Crusaders, one of the reasons that extremist groups had captured it and lured western forces into battle there. The Rome of Revelation was represented by the troops of the United Nations and the European Union.

"We're continuing to bait Allied troops," Cerastes said. "We captured some western reporters and we will be–"

"I don't need to know the details." The Cardinal held up his hand. It was much better not to know the atrocities that Cerastes had set in motion, although a few lives mattered little now.

After all, life was not about maximizing human wellbeing. It was about doing God's will and being His instrument to bring about the End Times. The serpent was just one of the important parts, a visible symbol of the end. Once events had gone far enough, the End Times would be declared and the Unbelievers would be punished.

The Cardinal knew that he would be the only one left standing. His faith was unshakeable. The Great Serpent would destroy these others and the world would be cleansed of the Unbelievers in the days after.

When he had first joined the Church, he had believed that the whole world could be saved and that somehow people would turn back to God. But over the years, he had seen enough to know that they just needed to start again. It was time for a purge, a cleanse, another type of Flood.

God's reset point on the earth.

"Ezekiel prophesied that fire and brimstone would rain down on the enemies of God's people," Echis said, interrupting his thoughts. "Have you organized the Allied troops?"

The Cardinal nodded. "If Cerastes amps up the atrocities, I can guarantee that there will be more bombs from the Allied forces. We will spark the tinder box, don't worry. The more violence in the Middle East, the more the fundamentalists claim the End Times. When the Great Serpent emerges, the battle will truly commence."

Echis grinned, his teeth glinting in the semi-darkness.

"Then we have much to do, brothers. I'll send word when the sarcophagus is here."

"The thousand years are ended." The men intoned the words together and then went their separate ways into the dark.

CHAPTER 17

Vatican City, Rome, Italy.

THE MENTION OF THE Pergamon Museum made Morgan start. It had only been a few nights since she and Jake had run through it to the Ishtar Gate to find the pictures that led them to the seal. Her anger still simmered at losing it again. With the attacks on her own family and then on Martin, Morgan was determined to beat Samael to the remaining seals.

The tourists crowded even closer as the guide ignored Morgan's small group in the typical Italian way and continued her talk.

"There are copies of the sculpture in many of the great museums of the world, including the Louvre in Paris, the Uffizi in Florence and the Grand Palace of the Knights of St John in Rhodes."

This last comment caught Morgan's attention.

The Knights of St John were also known as the Hospitallers, a medieval Catholic military order with a papal charter to defend the Holy Land. Unlike the Templars, who had been destroyed or at least driven underground by persecution in the fourteenth century, the Hospitallers persisted through history. Like the Church itself, they had survived the rigors of history and still protected secrets held since the Middle Ages.

This original Laocoon statue was such a tourist attraction within the walls of the Vatican that Morgan couldn't imagine how a seal could still be hidden here. But people didn't visit Rhodes for a replica of the Laocoon.

As the guide moved off, Morgan sidled back around the sculpture to Jake and Martin.

"Fancy a dip in the Aegean?"

* * *

Rhodes, Greece.

Morgan waited for Jake and Martin at a cafe on the edge of the harbor near the ruins of Our Lady of the Castle cathedral. The guys were sorting out accommodation and it was good to have a little time out. The pace of the ARKANE missions could be brutal and her bruises still smarted from the bombing at Delphi.

She looked out across the azure sea and sipped a cold Mythos lager, enjoying the refreshing fizz while the alcohol helped her relax. Rhodes was closer to Turkey than the mainland of Greece and the island was a haven for sun seekers, particularly as winter descended on Northern Europe. Morgan was grateful for a sliver of sun on her face. The climate here was similar to Israel and even the air smelled similar, salt fish on the breeze with a hint of citrus and olives. But she had no ties here, no memories and no chance of bumping into people she knew. Here she could pretend to be just a tourist, not a secret agent on the hunt for what might prevent the End of Days. Part of her wanted to melt into the tourist crowd, find a little place overlooking the ocean and just rest.

"Not a bad spot you've got here."

Morgan looked up to see Jake beaming down at her.

He'd changed and now wore a blue striped t-shirt and light chinos. He looked ridiculously good. Morgan smiled back.

"Glad you like it."

"I think more of our missions should involve Mediterranean islands." Jake sat down next to her. "Martin's back at the hotel room. He's calmer now so he's sifting through piles of ancient data on Near Middle Eastern seals. Fascinating stuff." He faked a yawn. "But we're field agents, so we need to be in the field." He gestured to the waiter for a beer. "Important agent things to be doing, after all."

He was quiet for a moment and they both looked out over the water, finishing their beers as they watched people stroll by. A couple stopped on the waterside in front of them, arms woven around each other. Their loving smiles were a glimpse into a relationship that Morgan found herself envying.

Jake cleared his throat. "Time to go?"

Together, they walked up the hill along the Street of the Knights towards the fortress, passing tourist trap shops along the way. The Palace of the Grand Master of the Knights of Rhodes was as imposing as its name, a medieval castle that towered above the town and the harbor, looking out over the ocean. Built in the Gothic Provencal style in the fourteenth century, two massive crenelated towers flanked the entrance. Silhouetted as they were against the blue sky, Morgan could easily imagine archers leaning over to shoot down invaders of old. The past was drenched in blood and the Catholic Church had shed more than its fair share. But then how different were she and Jake to the warrior priests of the Hospitallers?

They entered the gates into the inner courtyard. It was lined with a colonnade that offered shade from the hot sun.

"This is a pretty cool place." Jake's grin was infectious and Morgan couldn't help but smile back.

They walked into the inner fortress and entered the Great

Hall. A grand staircase filled one end of the room and at the top, Morgan could see the Laocoon replica. It overlooked the lobby in full view of the tourists below, who clumped together in a few groups around other areas of interest. Security guards were spaced out around the room and despite their Greek nonchalance and air of relaxation, they carried guns on their hips.

As they headed slowly towards the statue, Morgan took Jake's arm.

"Remember what you did at Santiago de Compostela?" she said in a quiet voice.

He nodded.

"I might need some kind of distraction like that again if I find something."

"Gotcha. I'll wait for your signal." Jake headed off in the opposite direction.

Morgan climbed the stairs towards the sculpture and a moment later, she stood in front of it. This Laocoon was clearly inferior to the original. It was a little smaller and although all the essential features were there, it was missing the smooth lines and the overall impact was less emotionally intense. Whereas the sculpture in the Vatican resonated with the death throes of a father trying to save his sons, this one merely seemed like decoration in a castle built for fighters, not art critics.

But there was something about it that puzzled her.

She examined it more closely, trying to remember the Vatican statue ... then she saw it. The altar that Laocoon the priest sat on was marked in a different way. There was a carving of a serpent on it, the ouroboros, the snake forming a circle with its tail in its mouth. Morgan couldn't recall seeing that on the Vatican statue. It looked like some kind of button.

She turned around and looked across the hall. Jake was standing on the other side facing her, right next to a painting of Hospitaller Knights marching towards Jerusalem. He had his head stuck in a guidebook but she could see that he was alert for her signal, watching her out of the corner of his eye. She nodded at him.

His shout rang out across the hall as Jake fell to the floor and began rolling around, faking an epileptic fit by the look of it. The guards turned towards the sound and ran to the balcony. Morgan only had a minute before calm would be restored.

She quickly turned to the statue and ran her fingers over the ouroboros. She pressed it hard and a little drawer sprung out the back with a small round package wrapped in dull ivory cloth inside. She picked it up, slid the drawer closed and put it in her backpack, then walked swiftly towards the exit. Behind her, security dealt with the continuing uproar as curious tourists huddled around the drama.

By the time Jake strolled back to the bar on the waterfront an hour later, Morgan had ordered two more beers and was halfway through hers. She looked up at his approach.

"Took your time." She pushed back a chair for him.

"I had to convince the nice doctors I was OK to leave."

"Nice work back there."

Jake gave a fake bow. "At your service. Now what did you find?"

Morgan pulled open her pack to show him the wrapped package. "It's definitely another seal. It matches the others."

"Do you really think these are the seals of Revelation?" Jake asked.

Morgan stared out at the blue ocean before them. She and Jake rarely talked about what they believed in terms of faith, but both of them had seen enough strange things to believe the seals could be real. "Patmos is only a few islands northwest of here."

Jake raised an eyebrow quizzically.

"That's where John, the author of the book of Revelation,

had his visions. Some say he was the apostle John, the one that Jesus loved, and the same author as the gospel of John. But textual analysis says otherwise. He was more likely a Christian exiled to the island during the persecution of Domitian. Father Ben once told me that he was likely in a fasting state when he wrote some of the visions but he certainly used a lot of Jewish prophecy in his work. Verses from the books of Daniel, Ezekiel, Psalms and Isaiah pepper the text."

"And the seals?"

Morgan shrugged. "Seven is a sacred number in various numerological traditions and it's used over 700 times in the Bible. Seven days to create the earth. The Sabbath is on the seventh day. There are seven hills in Jerusalem, and seven trumpets to sound the end."

"Seventh son of a seventh son."

"That's not actually in the Bible."

Jake grinned. "Iron Maiden is just as inspirational."

"What's puzzling me is who hid the seals," Morgan said. "If they are some kind of device that will open a sarcophagus, then why hide them near snake symbols?"

"Perhaps they were hidden by those who worshipped the serpent?" Jake mused. "Think about it. You've lost your sarcophagus. Some ancient do-gooders have buried it far away but you still have the seals. You know you won't live to see it opened but you trust that the Brotherhood of the Serpent, or whatever it's called, will eventually rise again and find the sarcophagus. So you hide the seals where they would know to look, in the very places that are sacred to the snake."

Morgan nodded. "Makes sense, I guess. So where's the next one?"

As she sipped her beer, Martin came scurrying along the waterfront, a sheaf of papers clutched in his hands. His shock of blonde hair stood up in clumps where he had been pulling it. The frown had deepened across his forehead, making him look much older.

He came to sit at their table and without so much as a hello, he thrust the papers at them, finger stabbing at an image on the top. "This must be it!"

CHAPTER 18

Rhodes, Greece.

MORGAN LOOKED DOWN AT the image Martin pointed at. It was a stone carving of a serpent curled around a circular object, its body wound through an ankh symbol. Next to it, the falcon god Horus wore the crown of Egypt and another cobra sat proudly at its feet. Martin stumbled excitedly over his words.

"The ouroboros you saw on the Laocoon, the snake eating its own tail. It's an ancient Egyptian symbol representing renewal and rebirth in the cycles of life. In the Book of the Dead, it's related to the god Atum who rose from the chaos of primordial waters in the form of a serpent. Later sources use it as a symbol in alchemy, linked to the Philosopher's Stone."

"Egypt?" Jake looked hopeful. "It's been a while since I've visited."

Morgan thought back to when Jake had lain in hospital, injured by the demon in the bone church while she had gone hunting for the Ark of the Covenant. Egypt had been a revelation, but also a place of violence and death, and she had no desire to return anytime soon. But it seemed she would have little choice in the matter.

"So where's this carving?" she asked.

"The goddess Wadjet, portrayed as an Egyptian cobra, is

on the wall of the Temple of Hatshepsut in Luxor," Martin said triumphantly.

"That circular object certainly looks like a seal." Jake peered more closely at the picture.

"It's a sun disk," Morgan said. She tipped her head on one side, trying to recall the symbolism associated with the goddess. "But I seem to remember that the first image of a snake curling up a staff was Wadjet shown as a cobra curling up a papyrus leaf in the pre-Dynastic era around 3100 BC. The symbol was later adopted by many Mediterranean cultures in various forms, such as the biblical graven serpent and the Greek caduceus."

"Exactly," said Martin. "I've run algorithms over the remaining cultures of the world that relate to snakes. But all the rest are much further away: the nagas in India and the Far East, the Rainbow serpent in Australia, and Quetzalcoatl in Central America. All these fall outside the parameters of what are considered likely to relate to the seals. But Egypt …" He shrugged.

Jake raised his glass to the setting sun.

"To Luxor next, then. But for now, I just want to finish this beer."

* * *

Grand Canyon Snake Valley Retreat, USA

Lilith knew she was taking too much of the venom, but increasingly she preferred the altered state of consciousness to her real life.

She spent her time curled up on top of the sarcophagus, crooning to the hidden life she knew pulsed beneath her. In her more lucid moments, she recognized that she was on the edge of what many would call madness. But something greater called to her. He whispered dark truths in the darkness and she listened, storing up the drips of poison in her heart.

Time seemed to both slow and pass like lightning. She barely ate and her ribs showed through the thin skin of her chest.

But she liked that.

She counted her ribs in the mirror every morning and watched the vertebrae of her backbone undulate. Although she had a pathetic thirty-three vertebrae and twenty-four ribs while the serpents had several hundred. Her body was inferior but it could still be useful. He had whispered that to her.

She would be His vessel.

She didn't know how, but she had to make sure she was there when the sarcophagus was opened. So she waited as if in hibernation in the darkness of the crypt. The time would come when she would act.

Lilith wasn't surprised when the door finally cracked open. The voices of men filtered down from outside and the sound of footsteps echoed through the vault. She rolled from the sarcophagus to stand in front of it. Her heart beat fast and she felt a little dizzy as she stood. She needed another shot of venom, but Samael had the vial she really wanted. Perhaps he had returned?

But it was Krait, the boorish security man, who walked down the stairs. He looked at her, his expression momentarily shocked before he hid his response.

In his eyes, Lilith saw a glimpse of what she had become. She must look like a physical wreck, but the man had no idea where her mind had been. He would be far too weak to take the venom trance.

She raised her chin, standing tall, her hand resting on the sarcophagus. But now she noticed the dirt under her nails and how ragged they were.

"What do you want?"

Krait pushed her aside. "Samael's orders," he said gruffly. "We're shipping the casket out of here. You're coming too." He glanced at her disheveled state. "Get changed and pack. We're flying to Israel this afternoon."

"Where's Samael?" Lilith asked, desperate for her next dose of the purest venom.

"Egypt," Krait grunted.

* * *

Luxor, Egypt.

The plane banked over the dark green curve of the Nile, and Morgan looked down on the ancient city of Thebes. It was an open-air museum and a mecca for any wannabe archaeologist. The massive temple complexes of Karnak and Luxor dominated the heart of the city. On the opposite side of the Nile lay the West Bank Necropolis, with the temples and tombs of the Valley of the Kings and the Valley of the Queens. Much had been discovered under the sands of the desert here, but surely much was still buried, hidden well and now forgotten. How little our lives matter in the grand scheme of history, Morgan thought. But that was comforting somehow, for when her body was dust, these magnificent monuments would continue to stand.

Unless of course, it really was the End Times.

She smiled to herself. As in all her ARKANE missions, Morgan battled her own scientific skepticism when it came to matters of faith. Despite what she had seen, she still clung to rational argument. Because if she became a true believer in the nature of evil and a supernatural battle was to come, then she might crumble. After all, what could one woman do against forces of that magnitude?

Jake snorted in his sleep. She looked sideways at him and Martin, both snoozing next to her on the plane. Well, one woman and two sidekicks.

If their foes were human and temporal, then they had a chance. She had to believe that. Those who wanted to use the seals to usher in some kind of apocalypse could still be stopped.

The plane touched down and they emerged into the bright sun of an Egyptian day. The air was like a furnace.

"It's good to be back in Africa." Jake smiled, striding down the stairs and stripping off his jersey to expose his brown arms to the sun.

Martin stood holding the railing, cupping a hand over his eyes to shield them. "It must be over forty degrees Celsius," he said in a weak voice, clearly wilting in the heat. "No one knows I'm here, so maybe I should just wait at the hotel for you to return? I could work on the possible locations for the final seal."

Morgan heard stress and deep fatigue in his voice, the longing for a cool room and some quiet time. They wouldn't be at the temple complex for long so he should be safe enough. She looked over at Jake. He nodded, concern for his friend visible in his eyes.

Morgan opened her pack and handed him the package from Rhodes. "You can keep this one safe for us too."

She was glad that Martin would be safe out of the way. The last time she had been in Egypt in the hunt for the Ark of the Covenant, things had gotten very dangerous indeed. She didn't worry about herself and Jake, but she hated to put Martin in danger. He wasn't cut out for fieldwork but until they knew who had shut him in the vault, he would be best off near them.

But maybe not too near.

They had told Marietti that Martin was here to provide backup in the field. The Director had sounded suspicious but he trusted them enough not to question what was going on. Clearly the threat was within the ARKANE organization itself, so the less he knew, the better.

After getting Martin settled at the Luxor Palace Hotel, Morgan and Jake caught a taxi over to the Mortuary Temple of Hatshepsut. It was a grand funerary complex, cut out of the towering cliffs at Deir el Bahari. As they drove up, a bank of cloud formed above the temple, casting dramatic shadows over the limestone cliffs as the wind whipped the air into an afternoon storm. Fat drops of rain spattered the earth. A roll of thunder rumbled in the distance.

"Storm's almost here," the taxi driver said, as he took their payment. "Better shelter inside."

Morgan and Jake ran the tourist gauntlet of the hawkers and headed up the long path to the temple, half jogging to get out of the rain until they reached the first level of colonnaded walkway. They turned to look back across the valley as rain pounded the dusty earth before them.

A crash of lightning split the sky, forking down onto the rocky plateau.

This place would have looked similar over three thousand years ago when they built it, Morgan thought. It was a spectacle of death in the Egyptian way, made even more resonant by the massacre of sixty-two people, mainly tourists, in 1997 by a fundamentalist group intent on disrupting the Egyptian economy. Layers of history piled up, alongside the bodies of those who died along the way.

As the rain eased, they walked out of the first colonnade and up the massive ramped staircase in the middle of the triple tiers to the second level.

"Hatshepsut ruled around 1500 BC," Morgan said. "The second historically confirmed female pharaoh. Her temple is dedicated to the sun god, Amun."

"It's pretty stark," Jake noted.

"It would have been hung with gardens back then,"

Morgan explained. "Frankincense and myrrh trees as well as many other foreign plants."

"So where's the carving?"

As they reached the top of the ramp, Morgan pointed through the colonnade to the inner temple. "Somewhere in there."

They walked through slowly, checking the walls as they went. Relief sculptures told the story of the divine birth of the female Pharaoh and an expedition to the exotic land of Punt on the Red Sea coast. There were statues of Osiris and columns with the cow-head of the goddess Hathor. But as Jake said, it was pretty stark with little personality.

"Her stepson, Thutmose III, destroyed a lot of the statues after her death," Morgan noted. "But once it would have been magnificent, an oasis in the desert. It's aligned to the winter solstice so the sunlight would pierce the inner temple and strike the statue of Osiris."

They walked around a corner and found an impressive wall of carvings in a sheltered niche. A vulture flew with wings outstretched, each feather detailed in blue and green with accents of crimson. Above it, eight cobras in strike pose inched along a frieze, each with a sun disk in a crown on their heads. It was stunning, but not what they sought.

After weaving around the temple behind a group of tourists, they finally found the carving, the original far more impressive than the picture Martin had showed them. Morgan imagined the chisel of the ancient sculptor, his hammer blows ringing out in the temple complex. The Egyptians were builders, that was for sure, and they were right in ensuring a physical memory. Walking lightly on the earth was all very well, and leaving no trace was an admirable philosophy, but what endured if no one built anything? And what would remain of the increasingly digital world when the silicon chips it ran on returned to dust?

"They don't make 'em like this anymore," Jake said, admiring the wall.

"They're still building the Sagrada Familia in Barcelona," Morgan replied. "You loved it there."

"Shame about the circumstance of our visit though." Jake frowned and Morgan knew he was thinking of the death of Santiago Pereira, the beginning of their hunt for the Key to the Gates of Hell not so long ago. He looked around them at the empty temple.

"I'm not sure where we're meant to hunt for this seal. The temple is almost stripped bare."

Morgan nodded. "I agree. Short of setting up a full archaeological survey, we won't find anything here. But there must be more images like this in some of the other tombs. Let's go and ask one of the guides."

Together they walked back to the tourist group who now milled around taking selfies with the colonnade as a backdrop. The guide stood in a corner, checking her phone. She looked up as Morgan and Jake approached and smiled in welcome.

"Can I help you?"

"We're looking for a portrayal of Wadjet, or some kind of serpent, in a tomb," Morgan asked.

"There are plenty of tombs around here." The guide smiled. "Can you be more specific?"

"Something unusual," Jake said. "Something that you wouldn't expect, rather than the usual cobra images."

The guide smiled up at him and thought for a moment. "Probably the best serpent in the valley is portrayed in Ramses I's tomb. It's in the Valley of the Kings, number KV16."

"Thank you, that's –"

Jake's words were cut off by the rattle of gunfire from the plaza below the temple.

Then the screaming started.

CHAPTER 19

THE GUIDE'S FACE WENT white with fear at the sound.

"Oh no, not again." She started shouting for her group. "This way, please. Follow me."

There were procedures in place since the terrorist attacks in the 1990s, but Morgan thought this was something different. As the tourist group streamed back through the colonnade, she and Jake slipped out to stand behind the pillars, shadowed by the darkness within. They looked down onto the lower level of the temple. A group of armed men cleared the area, herding the tourists away while another man stalked up the ramp towards them.

Morgan could just make out the snake tattoo on his neck. "Samael?" she whispered.

Jake nodded. "He must have had the same idea as us."

They slipped back into the temple, following the tourist group, hoping there really was another way out. Or pretty soon, Samael would make it up here and find them.

The guide led her group of tourists deeper into the heart of the temple and then veered right down a small tunnel. She pointed in front of her, herding them through.

"Quickly now," she whispered. "Follow the tunnel down. It's carved through the cliff behind us and emerges in the carpark at the Valley of the Kings."

The group ran down into the tunnel and eventually the

sound of gunfire faded, replaced by the dripping of water and the rasp of breathing as the tourists hurried away. Morgan and Jake stayed at the back, just in case anyone came after them.

But no one did.

As they walked down the tunnel, Morgan imagined Samael scouring the funerary complex for any trace of the seal. But he would come up short and likely head for the tombs of the other pharaohs next.

They had to stay ahead of him. She redoubled her speed.

Ten minutes later, the group emerged into the carpark, a wide tarmac area that held back the sands of the desert cliffs around them. The rain was heavier now and the guide corralled her tourists together, pointing them in the direction of coaches parked a little further away. Morgan and Jake turned towards the entrance to the Valley of the Kings, an unimposing start to the magnificence hidden inside the cliffs ahead.

Storm clouds whirled overhead and the rain intensified, hammering down. Morgan and Jake ran onwards, passing groups of tourists with colorful umbrellas heading back out again. The Valley of the Kings looked just like a load of caves cut into rock from the outside, but in the 500 years between the sixteenth and eleventh centuries BC, tombs had been dug here for the great pharaohs of the time. They ranged from simple pits to elaborate complexes, one with 120 chambers that would have been packed with precious objects for the afterlife. Each tomb was marked with a number. Sixty-three in all, most pillaged by grave robbers in antiquity, but Morgan was sure there was more to find in the desert out here.

By the time they found KV16, the tomb of Ramses I, Morgan and Jake were both soaked through.

"I love running in the rain." Morgan laughed as they ducked into the low tunnel.

"Definitely exhilarating." Jake grinned as they both dripped rainwater onto the cave floor.

The tomb was lit with dull electric lights. They attempted to preserve the incredible painting on the walls and ceiling, but also enabled the tourist horde to proceed without tripping over the rocky floor. At peak times, these tombs would be crowded with sweaty groups, flashing pictures while ignoring the No Flash signs and elbowing others out the way to get a better shot of the Egyptian funerary art. It was macabre tourism drawn here by the dead who had lain here for thousands of years.

But Morgan doubted that people would be so interested without Howard Carter and the curse of Tutankhamun. The discovery of the nearly intact tomb in 1922 sparked worldwide press reports and a renewed interest in Egyptology. The mysterious deaths of those involved had driven the hysteria even higher. The curse was considered by most to be complete fabrication, but the ancient Egyptians had certainly believed in magic. Supernatural forces still swirled about these places but Morgan didn't sense a threat here now. Even so, as they walked down the tunnel, it was clear that the paintings on the walls were meant to keep evil at bay, helping the dead into a happy afterlife.

After several chambers full of interesting paintings, Jake sighed.

"I'm having my doubts that this trip was worth it." He indicated the wall frieze. "Look at this. More servants with more grain and more animals to feed the Pharaoh in the afterlife, but no serpent."

"Just a little further," Morgan said, refusing to believe this was a wasted trip. Especially if Samael had the same idea.

Then they walked into the next chamber.

The wall painting portrayed a gold and green funerary barge. Slaves in white loincloths manned the oars while the Pharaoh sheltered under a canopy. Lines of hieroglyphics ran from top to bottom and Morgan could make out some symbols like the bird with a human head, known as the *ba*, the soul. Beneath the barge, a large serpent curled in six figure-of-eight loops, an intricate dance of death.

"Now that's what you call a serpent." Jake stepped closer to examine the detail.

"Its shape looks unnatural," Morgan noted. "More like a map. What do you reckon?"

"Could be. You want to go deeper into the tomb?"

Morgan nodded, a sense of excitement growing within her. At this point, they had nothing to lose. She took out her smart phone and took a picture of the curves of the snake.

They walked on through the tomb, quickly arriving at the first turn in the tunnel. There were two options. Morgan looked at the snake image and chose the left, following the undulations of its body.

Soon they reached a safety barrier indicating that the way ahead was closed and dangerous to proceed. A large stone had been rolled in front of the way to stop inquisitive tourists. Jake heaved it aside and they went on.

The lights grew dimmer as they continued following the turns, until only the light from Morgan's phone illuminated the way ahead.

"We must be almost there," she said. "One last turn."

They turned again and Morgan almost fell into blackness as her foot stepped onto air. She put her hand out to brace herself on the wall. Jake caught her round the waist, pulling her to him briefly.

"Careful," he whispered. "I don't want to lose you."

Morgan shone her light forward and down into a pit before them. In the middle was a stone altar with a smaller sarcophagus on top, carved with the undulating shapes of a serpent.

"We have to get down there." Morgan knelt down on the edge. "It's not too far. Can you lower me down?"

Jake held her hands and lowered her as far as he could. She dropped the last meter, landing with bended knees onto soft earth. It smelled damp, as if the rainstorm had found its way through the rock above, down to the chamber beneath. In a strange way, it felt more alive than the dusty tomb that the tourists visited, as if people had worshipped here more recently.

Morgan tried to pull the top from the smaller sarcophagus, but it was too heavy.

"Sorry," she called up to Jake. "You're going to have to come down and help me with this."

"Shine the torch over here."

Morgan turned the light to help him see his way down. He lowered himself as far as he could and then drop-rolled to the ground. Then he came over and heaved the top off.

"Good to know you can't do without me."

Morgan smiled. "Just making you feel useful."

She reached in and pulled out a stone roundel.

"This is it," Morgan whispered. "The sixth seal. It's beautiful."

The intricate carving of the snake wound around the circle, each scale perfectly cut. The others had suffered the ravages of time, but this one had been preserved down here.

With wide eyes, she handed it to Jake and he cupped it in his bigger hand, weighing it slightly.

"It's easier to believe the seals have some kind of intrinsic power when we're down here," he said quietly. "Or at least to think that someone once believed they did."

Suddenly they heard a scuffle in the tunnel above. Torchlight played along the walls, alighting briefly on the faces of the impassive gods.

Someone else was here.

Morgan looked at Jake with alarm. Together, they softly moved directly under the doorway.

"I know you're down there," an American voice called

from above. "And I know you have the sixth seal. But I have something you want too."

The sound of someone pushed to the ground. A groan of pain. Then the click of a gun.

"I'm so sorry." Martin Klein's voice filtered down to them in the dark of the crypt. "Please don't –"

A dull thud. A cry of pain, and Martin's words were cut off.

"I have the other seal and your friend. The question is how much do you value him?"

Jake stepped away from the wall with no hesitation. Morgan moved to his side and they both looked up.

"What do you want?" Jake asked.

Samael stood in the doorway at the top of the crypt. Martin knelt before him, face bloody and streaked with tears, one of his eyeglass lenses broken.

"Throw me the seal. You will have your friend back and I won't shoot all three of you. You're fish in a barrel down there, after all." Samael put his hand on his heart in a slightly mocking way. "You have my word."

Jake weighed the stone object in his hand. "This is the sixth seal, so there's still one more to find."

"True. But after I find it, the sarcophagus can be opened. Such a shame you won't be there to see it."

"Alright," Jake said. "On three."

Samael nodded.

"One, two, three."

On three, Jake threw the seal up towards Samael. The man caught it with one hand, but Martin remained kneeling at his feet.

"You gave your word," Jake said.

Samael laughed. "Of course."

He shoved Martin forward so he tumbled into the pit. Jake rushed forward to break his fall and the two of them ended up in a heap on the rocky ground.

"I promised not to shoot you, but you'll find the tomb sealed up for renovations, if you ever make it out of here. Perhaps the archaeologists of the next generation will find your bodies mummified down here." He smiled. "Now I'm going to retrieve the next seal." He started to walk away, then turned back. "You think those you love are safe, Morgan Sierra. I almost wish you could make it out of here to see that they are not."

He smiled and walked off, followed by his men. Their footsteps echoed up the tunnel. Moments later, there was the sound of a muffled explosion.

Samael had sealed the door.

They were trapped inside the tomb.

His last words echoed inside Morgan's mind. How could he be going after her family again? Faye and Gemma were safe inside ARKANE. Then she looked down at Martin, as Jake helped him dust off his clothes. They had gotten to him inside the vault, the heart of ARKANE London headquarters. So, how hard would it be to get to her family in Oxford?

She had to get out of here.

CHAPTER 20

MORGAN RAN TO THE wall below the doorway.

"Help me up!"

Jake leaned over and she put her foot into his hands. He boosted her and she sprang up, clambering back to the ledge above. She turned to call back to them.

"I'll go check the exit. Back in a minute."

Morgan ran down the tunnel the way they had come. Her heart hammered in her chest, not from the exercise but from the fear of what Samael planned for her family. Surely he couldn't get to them?

She made it to the safety barrier but as promised, the tunnel was blocked by a cave-in. They'd used enough explosive to bring it down but not enough to make sufficient noise to bring the guards. It was unlikely that the Egyptian authorities would check this far down into the tomb complex until morning.

"Help!" she shouted, hoping that somehow her cry would make it through the cavern. But the storm still hammered the valley outside, cloaking any sound. The tourists would all have gone back to their luxury hotels for the night, to be entertained with belly dancing and cocktails with pyramid-shaped ice. The guards would be huddled in their buildings, sheltering from the rain. There was no one to hear them. Samael had made sure of that.

Morgan banged her fist against the rock as she frantically considered the other options. They could explore the rest of the tunnels and look for another exit. But they might just end up lost in the caverns dug into the cliffs, their voices joining the whispers of the long dead. This was no time to go wandering away from the light.

She hefted one of the rocks away, her back muscles straining as she moved it just a few inches. Perhaps together they could shift enough to make a passage through.

Morgan jogged back to the pit and looked down at Jake and Martin. Their faces were ghostly in the semi-darkness and it was as if she saw them in the grave.

"The exit's blocked but we might be able to dig ourselves a way out. It's our only chance to get out of here before the morning security rounds."

Jake boosted Martin up and then clambered up after them himself. The three of them jogged back down the tunnel, their footsteps echoing through the chambers until they reached the barrier.

Jake raised an eyebrow. "He did a decent job of that." He turned to Morgan. "But at least you weren't under it this time." He bent his knees and hefted a rock up into his arms. "Guess it's time for a workout."

Morgan followed suit and Martin joined in, each of them working in silence punctuated only with the exhalation of breath.

An hour later, Morgan sank to the floor.

"Time out, guys."

Jake and Martin stopped shifting and sat near her. Jake wiped the sweat from his brow and looked over at the pile of rocks.

"We're making good progress."

Morgan laughed and shook her head. "Nice try, but we've barely touched it."

A knot of worry sat heavy in her stomach as she considered that they might not get out of here until morning when the security rounds began, or even when tourist groups arrived. There was no way they could shift all the rocks from the cave-in themselves.

"It's only six hours' flight from Luxor back to London." Morgan's frown deepened. "Samael could get to Oxford before dawn tomorrow."

"But the ARKANE labs there are pretty much impregnable," Jake said. "And when we fail to report in, Marietti will make sure your family is protected."

"Like he protected Martin in the crypt?" Morgan snapped back.

Martin huddled into the wall at her words, wrapping his arms around himself as if to ward off the truth.

"I'm sorry," she said with a sigh. "I'm just so worried."

Jake stood and walked over to where she sat. He sank down next to her and pulled her into a hug. There were no words that could help at this point, but Morgan was grateful for his support.

As they settled in for the night, she could only send positive thoughts to Faye, David and little Gemma. *Be safe. I'm coming as soon as I can.*

* * *

Oxford, England. The next morning.

Father Ben Costanza walked out of the Radcliffe Camera onto the square. He blinked a little as he emerged and breathed in the scent of the air after rain. The circular interior of the library was a haven in the middle of the busy city, part of the Bodleian Library. It held the theological texts he consulted in preparation for his lectures, although truth be told, he could have found them all online now. But he liked to get out of the hallowed hall of Blackfriars and feel part of the wider university. This was one of his favorite places, especially in the early mornings when no one else was around.

Sleep was a minor part of his life now and most nights he only rested for a few hours. One of the minor benefits of age perhaps, as he had more time to read and think. But this morning, he had woken while it was still dark with a sense of foreboding, a twisting in his gut that something was wrong. It had happened several times since returning from India, with nightmares of the Kali temple and a shadow of violent death that still lay heavy upon him. So he came here and had been deep in study since the early hours, but now he had to get back for a morning tutorial.

Ben loved his life at Oxford. After years of working for the Vatican, he enjoyed the relative freedom he had to pursue his studies as well as teach the next generation everything he knew.

Or at least some of it, he thought.

Much of what he had learned over the years was best left buried.

He gripped the handrail and slowly walked down the stone stairs, one step at a time. A couple of students bustled past him, laughing together as they strode towards their bikes, chained up in the tangle in the rack at the edge of the square.

Ben smiled to see them go, even though they didn't even notice him. The old were invisible, he thought. That had always been the way of things and he was more than ready to give way for the young. They would learn their lessons in time and he wished them many years before they faced the inevitable pain that would come.

Such was the wisdom of the old, Ben thought with a rueful smile, feeling the twinge of arthritis in his knees as he stepped down. The familiar pain heralded the beginning of autumn, when damp pervaded the stone wall of his rooms back at the college and seeped into his bones.

But autumn and winter had their own pleasures and he preferred Oxford in the darker days, dusted with snow, although that was rare these days. Mulled wine and Mass by candlelight, nights telling tales of old … and his books.

Always his books.

Despite the digitalization of the Bodleian Library and the march towards all things online, he still valued the weight of tomes filled with knowledge on his shelves. Amongst them, a rare Wettstein New Testament in Greek, a first edition of *The Pilgrim's Progress*, an illuminated Book of Hours from the Tudor period and an Armenian antiphony, a liturgical book used by the choir. Books he had collected on his travels in the Middle East, illuminated by the hands of monks long dead before him.

The many map books were amongst his most precious things, proof that borders meant nothing in the path of history. Most people assumed that countries were fixed, that nationalities were more than just an idea. But the map books Ben had on his shelves proved how the world had shifted over time, as men who cared more about resources like oil rather than people remade the borders to suit themselves. Maps proved the world was mutable, the edges porous, ever changing.

He thought of Morgan, off on another ARKANE mission. She worked on the edge of supernatural mysteries, as he himself had once done back in his Vatican days. He had thought those days were over, but on the trip to India, he had faced evil incarnate. He remembered the darkness of the Kali temple, the blood of sacrifice pooling before him and the thought that he would certainly be next.

He shivered and pulled his robe closer about him. He was glad to be back here, far away from the demons of the east. There were more than enough of his own to conquer.

Once on the main path, Ben shuffled along the cobblestones through the archway into the tiny square of the main Bodleian Library before walking out past the Sheldonian Theatre onto Broad Street. Students cycled past on their way to lectures, bells ringing to encourage the tourist photographers out the way. It was too easy to forget the glorious surroundings when hurrying to the next tutorial. The rarefied air of Oxford became just another city when an essay deadline loomed, and Ben supposed the romance of getting into the university soon faded with the reality of the workload.

But he was grateful for every day he was able to walk these ancient streets, for every moment he had left to breathe the air that so many brilliant scholars had before him. Time was ever more fleeting the older he became.

Would he swap his life for that of a newly minted student? Ben chuckled at the thought. No, he couldn't keep up with all the technology anyway and thank the Lord, he had a good life in these twilight years.

He turned at the church of St Mary Magdalen and walked past the Martyrs' Memorial, commemorating Anglican bishops Cranmer, Latimer, and Ridley, who had been burned at the stake in the sixteenth century. An unwashed man crouched on the steps, holding a bottle in a paper bag. The smell of booze emanated from his skin. He looked up as Ben passed, his eyes narrowing a little as if expecting some kind of reprimand.

Ben rummaged in his satchel for some coins and handed them to the man with a smile.

"For your supper."

It was hard being poor in a city like Oxford, where the elite were well catered to but the unfortunate of the city were unwelcome. Especially near the colleges.

Ben crossed the road to head up St Giles as he hummed

a few bars of Liszt's *Bénédiction de Dieu*. Outside the Ashmolean Museum, just before he reached the haven of Blackfriars, a white transit van swerved in.

It pulled up right next to him on the pavement. Ben stopped in surprise.

The door opened and a man jumped out, a tattoo of a snake winding up his neck.

Before Ben could even shout, the man shoved him through the side of the van, jumped in after and slid the door shut.

The van pulled out into the main road, heading north.

CHAPTER 21

Oxford, England.

BEN CLUTCHED AT THE sides of the van and pulled himself upright in the moving vehicle as it sped up the main road. The man sat watching him, his dark eyes unfathomable.

"What do you want, my son?" Ben asked.

"Father Ben Costanza." The man's tone was a threat. "Dominican monk based at Blackfriars. Tutor for the Angelicum, but once an archaeologist specializing in the Near East. Friend of the Vatican."

"Yes, all that is true." Ben nodded. "But what do you need from me?"

The man didn't blink. "Mentor to Doctor Morgan Sierra."

Ben froze at Morgan's name. He knew that her sister Faye and her family had gone into hiding with ARKANE in the last twenty-four hours but he didn't know the details why. Was this who she was running from?

The man smiled. "I see your fear, old man, but don't worry. If you help me, you need have no concern about your safety. Morgan Sierra has nothing I need now … but you do."

Ben sighed and shook his head a little. "I'm old and much of my life has been conducted in the shadows. I've traveled many places and seen many things. You'll have to be more specific."

The man nodded. "Soon."

The van turned sharp left and moments later, it turned down a bumpy road. Ben considered where they might be. Given the short distance, it was likely they were in the more rural area near Wolvercote. It was close to the city but there were still farmhouses that seemed in the middle of nowhere.

There would be no one to hear him shout for help.

His tutorial student would wait ten minutes and then take advantage of his absence to go work on his essay again. No one would miss him until tomorrow's breakfast when the professors, monks and students gathered in the Hall. Even then, sometimes he skipped it when fasting. He was at the mercy of this man for at least twenty-four hours.

But it couldn't be any worse than the Kali temple. An image of Sister Nataline flashed through his mind, how her faith had sustained her even as she faced certain death.

Could he be so brave? Would he have to be?

The van stopped and the man pushed the door back to reveal a small cottage on the edge of a wide-open green field. Port Meadow, the closest Oxford came to wilderness, a large area of common land recorded in the Domesday Book of 1086 … and a haven of peace and quiet. Nothing like the busy city only a few kilometers away.

The man got out and reached in a hand to help Ben clamber down. Another man emerged from the front of the van and went to open the cottage door.

"We won't be disturbed here." Ben heard the edge of threat in his voice. "Krait," the man called. "Prepare the room."

Ben balked at the words, but there was nowhere to run and they would soon catch him even if he could break away. His old legs were not meant for much more than hobbling these days.

But at least he could go with some dignity.

Ben stood tall, shaking the man's hand from his arm. He

walked towards the door, trying to be steady on his feet. He'd seen Morgan fight before and for a moment, he toyed with the idea of channeling her strength. Perhaps he could get away from the man.

He saw a spade by the edge of the garden. It was only a few paces away on the diagonal. The edge was sharp and he could swing it as a weapon.

"Don't even think about it," the man behind him growled. "Go inside."

Ben stepped under the ivy-clad doorway into the cottage. Deep grey flagstones led into a homely kitchen, but the place smelled musty and unused.

The other man, Krait, stood inside. He waved a hand towards the sitting room. Ben turned in and gasped at the sight.

A wooden chair had been placed in the middle of the room and the floor covered with black plastic. Beside the chair was a small table with a series of knives laid out upon it.

He grabbed hold of the door, backing away.

"No, please!"

Krait forced him forward.

* * *

Valley of the Kings, Egypt.

The clunk of metal on stone and the yammering of voices woke Morgan from a restless sleep filled with nightmares. She opened her eyes to see a chink of light appearing at the top of the cave-in.

She rolled to her feet and clambered up, trying to see out of the crack.

"Help! We're trapped in here."

An Egyptian security guard appeared at the hole.

"I'm so sorry, miss. This is terrible. Please move away from the rocks and we'll have you out soon."

Morgan slid back down to the bottom of the pile. Jake rubbed his eyes as he got to his feet. Martin uncurled himself from the floor, stretching his stiff limbs. The sound of the rescuers grew louder as they redoubled their efforts to clear the way.

"Hopefully it won't take them long to get us out of here," Morgan said. She felt a dawning sense that everything could possibly turn out OK. The Egyptian authorities were very concerned that tourists had a good experience here and after gunfire at the Hatshepsut temple yesterday, it was likely that they wanted to prevent any further negative press. They would hurry.

She looked at her watch, calculating the time in England. She imagined Gemma waking up, the little girl reading one of her favorite books in bed with her cuddly toy dog. Faye would be there, arms around her daughter. Morgan smiled at the thought and then her smile faded. If Samael touched them … she couldn't bear to consider it.

She picked up another rock and hefted it away from the pile. Jake and Martin joined in, redoubling their efforts. She had had quite enough of being trapped in caves.

* * *

It was another hour before there was enough space for them to squeeze out the top of the cave-in into the chamber beyond. Morgan slid down the other side into the waiting arms of the Egyptian security team. There were medics on site who insisted on checking them for any injury.

"I'm fine, really. I just need a phone."

As a medic cleaned some of her superficial injuries,

Morgan managed to get a mobile from one of the security guards. She called Marietti and the Director answered on the first ring.

"Damn it, Morgan. Where have you been?"

She quickly told him what had happened.

"But we're all fine. It's my sister I'm worried about. Samael threatened those I love."

"Just a minute. Hold the line and I'll check."

Marietti kept the phone line open so she could hear him call the Oxford ARKANE labs. One of the agents answered and Morgan heard the rumble of low voices, but couldn't quite make out the words. Then Marietti came back on the line.

"They're OK. Gemma slept well and she's having break-fast. Faye and David are coping well despite the shock of the attack. They're safe. I've told the agents to activate the shut-down protocol until further notice. No one is getting in there."

Morgan sighed with relief, the weight of concern lifting a little. But how many more times could she put her family in danger? Was her role at ARKANE just too risky for those she loved?

Then a cold fear tightened around her heart.

"Ben," she said. "Is he safe too?"

Marietti was quiet for a moment. "He refused extra security when we returned from India," he said. "But let me see if we can locate him."

Once again, Morgan heard his low voice, but this time there was a darker tone.

"He's not in his office and he didn't show up for breakfast, but the Porter says he often works at the Rad Cam in the early mornings. I'll send someone to find him, Morgan. You just get to the airport and come home."

As he cut the line, Morgan sat unmoving in the tomb as the medic swabbed her wounds. The smell of antiseptic filled the air, the hubbub of voices around her as security teams tried to get everything under control. But she could only see the wall in front of her, a portrayal of the death of the Pharaoh, his heart weighed against the feather of truth as he left this world for the one beyond.

CHAPTER 22

Oxford, England.

KRAIT PUSHED BEN INTO the chair as the other man entered the room behind them. Together, they bound him, arms pinned by his sides, legs taped to each chair leg, a final piece of tape over his mouth.

Then they left the room.

Ben broke out in a cold sweat as he looked at the table of knives by the chair. His heart beat so fast he thought it might burst from his chest. Lord, give me strength. Martyrs had suffered torture and pain for the sake of Christ. They were in glory now. If he could just calm himself ... but his eyes kept lighting on the knives and he could almost feel the sharp edges on his flesh. This body was old and he feared that he would not be strong enough to withstand the pain.

What did the man want?

Ben wracked his brain for something that they could be interested in but the years jumbled together in his mind, the many archaeological digs he'd been on, the artifacts he'd worked with at the Vatican, the people he had wronged along the way. He had sought forgiveness, praying for his own soul and those of others, but all leave a wake in the path through life. Sometimes those ripples have unintended consequences.

The sharp whistle of a boiling kettle pierced the air.

A minute later, the first man entered the room with two steaming cups. He placed one on the table next to Ben, alongside the knives.

"Hot, sweet tea. Helps with stress. Can we talk a little?"

Ben nodded.

The man pulled the tape away and lifted the cup for Ben to sip. Sweetness filled his mouth and the taste calmed him a little. The man wiped a little dribble from his chin, an almost tender gesture.

"Forgive my brutal tactics but I'm going to be honest with you, Ben. We don't have much time. So we need to begin now and I need you to cooperate. I hope I don't have to use these." He nodded to the knives. "Let's begin with introductions. My name is Samael."

His words sent a chill down Ben's spine. The archangel of death, the seducer and destroyer. For a man to take such a name, he had to be committed to the dark.

"I seek the seven seals of Revelation."

Ben paled. It was worse than he had thought.

Samael took up one of the knives, his hand hefting its weight.

"I dislike such crude measures of torture, so I have something that will help you remember. Something that will make your compliance pleasurable." Samael walked out of the room and then returned a minute later with a hypodermic needle. The liquid within was a pale green. "Your kind have always been wannabe martyrs, resisting pain with the power of faith. But with this, you won't be able to control your response. Even your God won't be able to stop you speaking of the past."

Ben squirmed on the chair, pushing himself as far away as he could but he was pinned.

Samael advanced towards him and pulled Ben's collar down. He grabbed Ben's hair and yanked his head sideways. He plunged the needle into the muscles of his neck.

Ben felt the sting and then pressure as the liquid forced into him, burning like fire as it spread.

"This is a hallucinogen distilled from the venom of the coral cobra, one of God's most beautiful snakes, with distinctive red and black bands." His voice was mocking. "There is no cure for the venom but this is just a tiny dose." Samael pulled the needle from Ben's neck. "You might even enjoy the experience, as it dulls the real world around you."

Samael sat back in the chair opposite Ben and sipped his tea as he waited for the poison to take effect. Minutes ticked past and it seemed that the silence expanded to consume the space. All Ben could hear was the dry rustle of snakeskin across the floor behind him.

Or did he imagine that?

Samael's dark eyes raked his soul and Ben felt that the man saw something inside him, the darker part, the aspect of himself he wrestled to deny, that he prayed on his knees to subdue.

But all men had a drop of darkness within them and Ben felt the poison caressing that part of him, a tendril of truth after a lifetime of hiding.

He wanted to confess. He wanted to give up the secret he had held for so long.

"I found a seal." Ben heard himself from a long way off. It didn't even sound like his own voice anymore. "On a dig in Ephesus many years ago." His mind slipped back into the past, back to the days when he was young and he was in love with Marianne, Morgan and Faye's mother. He had watched her that summer and doubted his calling to the Church. But she had loved another.

"Continue." Samael's voice snapped through his memory.

"I was part of a series of digs, investigating what was left of the seven churches named in Revelation. The Vatican believed that much of the book wasn't allegory but real. We found seven lampstands in the ruins. And although there weren't seven seals, I did find one."

"Where is it now?" Samael snapped.

"I didn't give it to the Vatican like I should have." Ben's voice trailed off.

Samael slapped him across the face, the jolt of pain anchoring Ben to the here and now. "I don't have to hurt Morgan and her family, but I will. Answer me."

Ben couldn't remember why he ever thought to hide the seal, but whatever the reason, it was nothing compared to those he loved. He was at the end of his own days, and theirs were just beginning.

"It's in the Ashmolean," he whispered. "Within their extensive catalogue of ancient Near Eastern seals, hidden in plain sight. No one would think it was anything special and when they collected other seals from the period, I donated it."

"Why is it special?"

Samael bent close. Ben could see each scale of his snake tattoo, the pulse in the vein in his neck giving it a semblance of life.

He frowned. It was important not to say the words but he couldn't resist. The venom freed his tongue. Perhaps this was God's will anyway. He was a mere wisp in the wind, blown apart by forces much bigger than himself. He took a deep breath and uttered the words he had never before spoken aloud.

"I fear it is one of the seven seals that will usher in the End Times."

As he said the words, Samael smiled with triumph and began to free him from the chair.

"Krait," he called. "Get the van. We're going back into Oxford."

Ben couldn't move. His head rolled onto his chest as the bonds loosened. His limbs felt disconnected, as if they weren't his own and he was dimly aware that his heart rate was much faster now, his pulse skipping beats. He heard it thudding in his chest like a countdown.

As the two men helped half-drag, half-carry him to the van, Ben realized that hours had passed. The night air smelled of autumn leaves and a hint of wood smoke. With his heightened senses, he could separate the scent of decaying flowers in the mulch of the earth from the tang of his own cold sweat. He could feel the muscles of the men by him and sense his own wasted body. The filters of reality shifted and for a moment, Ben felt as if his own flesh melted into theirs. He was just a tiny part of a whole organism. Wonder flooded his mind.

Krait pulled open the door and they lifted him inside the van, laying him on the floor.

Ben could feel the cool metal against his skin, a welcome balm to his heated flesh. Visions of the martyrs from history came to him and flames danced across his flesh as they drove back into Oxford. But his eyes were fixed in another realm and he smiled at the sheer beauty of it.

In what seemed like moments later, Samael and Krait walked him into the delivery entrance round the back of the Ashmolean.

"Is he alright?" a gruff voice said. One of the security guards, clearly paid off to let them in.

Samael pulled a wad of cash from his pocket, the roll of hundred pound notes silencing the guard. They walked on.

Now that he was inside, Ben felt pulled to the seal, as if it called to him through the museum corridors.

He had been in to visit it over the years. It always pleased him to see it sitting side by side with seals used for official correspondence, the disinterested public not seeing the true meaning of the stone. The gaudy and shiny objects attracted more attention. As it was with so much of life.

"That way," he panted and his words seemed to linger in the air.

Ben led Samael and Krait into the labyrinth of corridors. Like so many great museums, the Ashmolean was an overwhelming cornucopia of ancient delight, a treasure trove of objects, each of which had a story spanning generations. Ben had spent many of his days here over the years, as it was just next door to Blackfriars and he enjoyed the company of strangers without having to talk to them. The sense of history soaked through the walls of the place. The colors around him were brighter now and Ben wished he could stop to look once more at some of his favorite objects.

But there was no time.

He led Samael and Krait to the ancient Near Eastern section and stopped in front of a glass-fronted case.

"It's that one." Ben pointed at a round stone seal with the undulating curves of a serpent clearly visible on its surface. He remembered digging it from the ground of Ephesus that summer, a symbol of an ancient belief that even pre-dated Christianity. Now he could feel the tightening of the serpent's coils.

It was suddenly hard to breathe.

Ben sank to the floor, clutching at his chest through a haze of pain. He watched as Krait pulled a crowbar from his backpack and hammered the metal into the glass.

It cracked. An alarm rang out.

"Hurry!" Samael shouted. Krait smashed the glass again, then levered the end of the crowbar into the hole and pulled the shards away.

Samael took the seal from its case, a triumphant smile on his face. "The seventh seal."

At his triumphant words, Ben felt a jolt of pain flash through his chest. In the depths of the venom trance, he sensed his end approach.

It was past time.

He summoned Morgan's face to his mind, the daughter he never had, the woman he was so proud of. There was only one thing now that might stop the Great Serpent from consuming the world. He hoped she would find it.

But he could do no more.

A violent spasm wrenched Ben into blackness.

CHAPTER 23

As dawn broke over London, Morgan looked out of the plane window at the sleeping city nestled around the curves of the River Thames below. Millions of people lay down there with no idea of ARKANE and the secrets they kept, no clue about the edge of destruction averted so many times. She had once been one of those unknowing, and now she could never go back to that state.

Even if she left and returned to her university position in Oxford, she would always be aware that Jake and the other ARKANE agents walked the earth, hunting down dark secrets.

She looked over at Jake now, his face relaxed in sleep, the corkscrew scar the only physical evidence of the battles he had faced. Could she really have a normal life on the outside?

As the plane touched down soon after, Morgan turned her phone back on. When they had boarded the plane a few hours ago, Marietti still hadn't located Father Ben and she had spent the flight worrying. She hoped he was lost in some manuscript in one of the lesser-known libraries around the university, head bent over ancient Greek words. He had forgotten the time, that was all. Just an old scholar lost in his manuscripts. But she also felt a rising sense of desperation, and she held back her tears as her phone beeped.

There were several voicemails and a text message.

Morgan's heart beat faster as she opened it.

There's a car waiting for you at Arrivals. You need to get to Oxford.

She took a deep breath, trying to calm herself.

Ben was more than a mentor. He had been her mother's friend a long time ago and when her parents divorced, Ben supported Marianne and helped her care for the twin daughter, Faye, that she left behind when she died of breast cancer. Morgan had met Ben later in life and he had helped her settle in at Oxford, providing guidance to the academic political quagmire.

He had helped her and Jake on so many ARKANE missions, risking his life for her in the flames of the Grand Lodge of the Freemasons and almost dying in India in the hunt for the Shiva Nataraja statue. He was an old man, for sure, but he had an inner strength that made him seem so much younger.

Morgan summoned Ben's face to her mind, his quiet smile, the depth of his faith despite what he had seen in the darker side of religion. It was never God who erred in his mind, only His creation.

Jake stirred and opened his eyes. He frowned as he saw the concern on her face.

"What's wrong?"

"It's something about Ben." Morgan clicked the voicemail button and listened to Marietti's words, color draining from her cheeks as she heard what had happened.

Morgan, I'm so sorry. Father Ben was found at the Ashmolean Museum next to an exhibit of Near Eastern seals. He died of a massive heart attack and his body showed signs of poisoning by snake venom. One of the seals is missing. We're sure that Samael and the Brotherhood of the Serpent were involved.

"No!" Morgan couldn't help her cry of despair. Tears welled up and ran down her cheeks. Jake pulled her close, rocking her as Marietti's voice continued the message.

His body is at the John Radcliffe hospital morgue. The car waiting at Arrivals will take you straight there. Again, I'm so sorry. Despite our differences, Ben was a good man. Call me when you can.

Morgan wept as Jake held her. He said nothing while she sobbed and for that she was grateful. Sometimes, there were no words.

The worry and pain of the last few days overflowed and Morgan let it all out. Not long ago, she had fought for Ben's life in a bloody temple in India. She had expected many more years together, and now he was gone.

Her tears finally slowed and Morgan felt the stirrings of a white-hot anger. She raised her head and wiped her eyes.

"Samael will pay for Ben's death." Her voice was calm. "I'm going to Oxford to say goodbye and then we'll track the bastard down."

Jake nodded. "Do you want me to come with you?"

"No. I need to do this alone. Can you work with Martin on where Samael might be going next? If he has all seven seals, we need to find where he's planning to use them."

* * *

A few hours later, Morgan arrived at the John Radcliffe Hospital in Oxford and headed for the morgue. Although Ben's body had been identified already, Marietti had arranged for her to visit before it was released to the funeral directors.

The clinical white corridors smelled of antiseptic, an attempt to reverse the stench of sickness and decay of death. The scent took her back to the tomb in the Valley of the Kings. Death comes for all in the end and cannot be held back for long. Ben had been old, and of course, Morgan had expected this day would come at some point. She had hoped he would go to his God in his study surrounded by books, in the comfort of the life he had built for himself. But then few are able to choose the manner of their own deaths.

She entered the morgue and signed in, before being escorted to the viewing area. In a small white room, a body lay on a metal gurney under a white sheet, face covered.

Now she was here, Morgan hesitated.

She had seen death so many times, but this was different. After her own father had been blown up in what had seemed like a suicide bombing in Israel years back, Ben had been like a second father to her. She couldn't bear the thought of seeing his face now, lifeless on a slab.

Morgan steeled herself. She needed to be sure, and she owed Ben these last moments. She walked to the body, and stood by the head. She nodded and the lab tech pulled the sheet down, revealing the face of the corpse.

Ben's face.

Tears sprang to her eyes and ran down her cheeks as Morgan looked down on his dear features one last time. White hair swept back from a strong brow. Lines that had been earned through living and working hard for his God. She didn't know too much about Ben's past but she knew that he had given much for his belief. And he would have done anything for her.

She took one last look, understanding that this physical body wasn't the man she had loved, just his temporary shell. The Ben she knew had gone.

"Thank you."

The lab tech covered him again. Morgan turned and walked out. She would remember Ben as he was in life. At his funeral, the remains of that physical body would be lowered into the ground, but his kindness and faith lived on in her memory. She would honor that.

She would also make sure that the man who sent him to his grave would beat him into the ground. She would find Samael.

First, she needed to check Ben's office. Martin had sent through security footage showing Ben being taken from St Giles and many hours later, being escorted through the halls of the Ashmolean. A seal had been stolen, but Morgan was puzzled as to how Ben knew about it.

She needed to get to his rooms before the college cleared them out.

A short time later, Morgan arrived at Blackfriars, her heart heavy. Tears pricked her eyes as she walked towards the staircase that led to Ben's study rooms. She passed the green quadrangle where students lay on the grass, laughing and joking together. The sound rang hollow for her, even though she knew that Ben kept his window open so he could hear the students. They kept him young, he always said.

"Dr Sierra?"

The voice came from the window of the Porter's Lodge. Morgan turned to see an old man dressed in a three-piece suit poking his head out and waving at her. Fred, the Porter, took his job as the gatekeeper to the college very seriously.

She hadn't signed in. Morgan walked back over.

"Sorry, Fred. I'm just here to visit Father Ben's room one last time. Is that OK?"

"Of course. And you know how sorry we all are to hear of the Father's passing. He was a good man. With the Lord now though. A better place."

Morgan didn't share Fred's faith but she nodded. "I'm going to miss him so much."

Fred reached a hand out and squeezed her shoulder. "He certainly thought a lot of you, Dr Sierra. In fact, he told me to give you something. It was a while back, before he went to India. He must have been worried about traveling at his age, I s'pose." Fred opened a tall filing cabinet and rustled around in the papers. He pulled out a manila envelope and handed it to her. "He said that if anything happened, I was to give you this."

Her name was written on the front in Ben's handwriting.

"Thank you. Do you mind if I read it up in his room?"

Fred waved her away. "Take as long as you like. We're not scheduled to get the room cleaned up until after the funeral at the end of next week."

Morgan walked back across the quad and up the stairs to Ben's room. She pulled a key from her pocket and opened the door. It was dark inside and she went to pull the curtains open. The room smelled of cinnamon and nutmeg, the spices of the chai tea that Ben loved so much. She took a deep breath and closed her eyes, hoping to feel him here somehow.

But Ben was gone.

Morgan opened her eyes and looked around at his study, dominated by shelves piled with books. Ben had never defined himself by physical possessions, but he certainly loved to read. She had sat here so many times asking him convoluted theological questions and he had always pulled down exactly the right tome to find the answer. He had retained his quick mind and inexhaustible memory to the end.

Who would she ask her questions of now?

Martin Klein? Google?

Morgan smiled at the thought. Then she looked down at the letter in her hand. She sank down to the chair and opened the envelope. It contained one sheet of paper covered with Ben's spidery handwriting.

My dearest Morgan,

I write this as I head to Goa to meet you. The Lord only knows what we shall face together this trip. Part of me is excited to join you on a mission! But time passes and I grow weaker and I worry that I won't have time to tell you what I need to. So this letter is just in case and if you've reading it, then I am gone.

Don't be sad that I've passed beyond the veil. I've been so tired these last years so it will be a relief to go, although I will miss seeing your future triumphs. And they will be triumphs, dear Morgan, whatever you choose to do. I will miss seeing little Gemma grow up and I hope you and Faye will nd your peace with each other.

Take whatever you want from my study, whatever will help you or leave it all. It matters not.

Except one thing.

There is a box that is for you and you alone. Do not tell ARKANE of it for I know that Marietti would dearly love what is inside. Remember the day we discussed the role of Spirit-inspired prophecy vs. the effect of fasting in the Revelation of St John? You will nd the directions in the book we talked of then.

Be safe, Morgan, and know that I have always loved you as the daughter I could never have.

Ben

Morgan let the silent tears come as she re-read his words. At his age, the end could have come at any time, and Ben had been ready to face it. But he should not have died in agony without those he loved around him, and her rage would not abate until she avenged his death.

But first, she had to find this box and her curiosity was piqued as to what could be within. ARKANE had vaulted rooms under Trafalgar Square in London, containing precious objects from all cultures across history. What could Ben have kept that ARKANE could possibly want? She knew that Ben and Marietti had a history together, a distrust from their past at the Vatican and both kept secrets she would never know. She smiled. Trust Ben to leave a mystery, knowing she would be unable to resist the hunt.

She looked up at the wall-sized bookshelf and tried to remember the conversation he referred to. It was a few winters ago, before she had even joined ARKANE. She had a client at her private psychology practice, a survivor of a cult. The girl had believed the End Times prophecy, but much of their cult practice involved extreme periods of fasting. Morgan had gone to Ben to understand his perspective, since fasting was a common spiritual practice in many religions and Ben specialized in multi-faith disciplines.

She stood and scanned over the titles, running her fingertips along the oversize spines.

This one.

She pulled the book from the middle shelf, a treatise on fasting by Rabbi Jonathan Sacks. Not a book that many would expect in the library of a Dominican monk.

There was something in the pages and as she shook the book, a postcard fell to the floor.

Morgan picked it up. There was no writing on it but the distinctive spire of the building on the front caught her eye.

CHAPTER 24

Salisbury, England.

MORGAN AND JAKE WALKED down the path through the expansive green lawn around Salisbury Cathedral. The tallest spire in Britain towered over the town, and Morgan looked up as they approached.

"It was built in the thirteenth century to the glory of God," she said quietly, "but there are a lot of interesting things about this place."

"Stonehenge is only up the road a little way, isn't it?"

The prehistoric standing stones were thirteen kilometers north, constructed over 4000 years ago as a pagan worship site aligned with the sunrise of the summer solstice and the sunset of the winter solstice. Like the Egyptian temples, light would strike a particular stone on a particular day, evidence of the continuation of the gods' pact with mankind.

Morgan realized that Jake was trying to distract her from dwelling on Ben's death. She appreciated his attempt, but truthfully, this place really was fascinating. While Martin worked on trying to locate the sarcophagus, they had some time and Salisbury was only a few hours' drive. Martin had relocated to the vaults below Oxford, and promised to keep an extra eye on Faye and Gemma. While Morgan wanted to go to them, she needed to finish things with Samael first to ensure they would be safe. She would not see her sister's face on a mortuary slab.

"This cathedral, the church of Old Sarum, and Stonehenge are said to be placed on a ley line," she said. "They're considered by some to be ancient trackways of pagan Britain, mystical alignments that have a certain energy."

Jake raised an eyebrow. "Sounds like fun. What are we expecting to find here?"

"Ben's note implied some kind of box, but your guess is as good as mine as to where it might be. Or what's inside."

They continued up the path towards the church. The Great West Front portico featured sculptures of the patriarchs, prophets, apostles and saints, many heavily weathered over time. Morgan recognized Abraham with his knife, Daniel with a lion at his side, and a horned Moses with the tablets of the law. There were even some women, Saint Katherine with the wheel she was martyred on, Saint Barbara with a palm and castle. In the Jewish faith that Morgan was raised within, such images were never used, but she had to admit that these churches were spectacular. A myriad of stories in stone.

Some of the more weathered sculptures had been replaced with newer statues and Morgan was surprised and pleased to see one with clearly African features, evidence that Salisbury Cathedral moved with the times. After all, the church was far more active in sub-Saharan Africa, Latin America and Asia these days than it was in the historic centers of Europe.

She consulted the notes that Martin had provided about the church.

"That's Canon Ezra Baya Lawiri," she said, indicating the sculpture. "A Sudanese teacher who translated the Bible into the local Moru language. He was killed in the Sudanese war in 1991."

"I don't think I've ever seen an African face carved on an English cathedral," Jake noted, smiling up at the serious figure clutching his Bible. "It's incredible to think that they didn't have the Bible in their language until he translated it so recently."

They walked through the great door into the cathedral, emerging into the colonnade of the cloisters. Arched stone windows looked onto a square lawn beyond with a massive cedar tree dominating the space. With the rain dripping down outside, it was peaceful but there was a chill here too. Morgan imagined the faithful coming here over the last 800 years, walking the cloister quadrangle as they prayed for their health, for enough to live on, for the safety of their families. People weren't so different now, although perhaps more distant from the spiritual energy of a place like this. But the stone had soaked up the faith of years and Morgan could still feel the imprint of the past here.

They walked into the cathedral nave and stood for a moment at the back. It had a Gothic vaulted ceiling, the lines of the arches accentuated by the use of darker grey Purbeck marble against lighter Chilmark stone walls. Light streamed through stained glass windows either side.

A modern font in the shape of a curving Greek cross reflected the high ceilings above. Biblical sayings ran around the edges. *When you pass through the waters, I will be with you.* Isaiah chapter forty-three. So often these Christian churches used words from the Jewish scriptures and the simple use of water made Morgan feel closer to God than the grand architecture around them. Any belief she did have was rooted in the needs of a desert people, and water was always precious.

They walked on past the niches that lined the nave where noblemen had been buried over the years. Morgan glanced into each of the side chapels as they passed. She didn't know what they were looking for, but she trusted Ben enough to know she would recognize whatever it was when they found it.

They walked down to the far end of the cathedral. A

stained glass window in hues of deep blue and shades of red cast a darker light onto a small altar. A candle wrapped in barbed wire stood before it, representing Prisoners of Conscience imprisoned for their faith around the world. It was striking, but not what they were looking for. They continued on in front of the choir stalls, emerging before the altar. It was simple, a juxtaposition to the ornate stone and wood carvings around it.

Then Morgan glanced up.

"Oh!" She couldn't help the exclamation of surprise as she caught sight of the strange window above the altar. She pointed up to a series of glass panels.

Moses stood in the center, a golden serpent wrapped around a pole next to him. At his feet, people lay on the ground writhing in pain while snakes slithered around them. Underneath, they could faintly make out the words, *Even so must the Son of Man be lifted up*, from John's gospel, chapter three.

"That is a strange image to have above a Christian altar," Jake said.

"I know," Morgan replied. "I've never seen the brazen serpent image used in such a prominent place before. The book of Numbers, chapter twenty-one recounts that God told Moses to make a bronze serpent so that any who were bitten could be healed by it. As we saw at Megiddo, the snake was a cultic object in ancient Israel. There was a serpent in the Holy of Holies, known as Nehushtan, before the reforms of Hezekiah, before the First Temple was destroyed. The serpent was also known in other ancient cultures as having healing properties."

"Like the rod of Asclepius in ancient Greece."

"Exactly. But it's strange because graven images were considered anathema to the Jews. They were punished for the golden calf in the desert, and yet this snake remained a symbol. And now the church uses it as an analogy for Jesus."

Jake frowned. "It's a bit of a stretch to compare Jesus to a serpent, isn't it?"

Morgan nodded. "I've always thought so, although perhaps it relates to healing in some way. A supernatural remedy for snakebite is something truly precious to a desert people."

"So what's the significance? Why would Father Ben send us here?"

Morgan's face crumpled at Jake's words and he reached out a hand to grasp hers.

"I'm sorry," he said softly.

Morgan wiped the tears from her eyes. "I miss him so much already, but I'm determined to find what he left me. Samael is mine when we find him, Jake."

He nodded. "Understood."

Morgan looked up again at the stained glass. "We need to ask who worked on this or whether there are any other artifacts that relate to the serpent here."

They walked back down the nave and into the little shop at the side of the cloisters. Morgan spoke to one of the ladies serving and they were directed back towards the document archives.

An elderly man met them at a rickety desk.

"We're interested in the Moses window," Morgan said. "I think a friend of mine had something to do with it. Father Ben Costanza?"

The man's eyes didn't flicker. Morgan saw no indication that he recognized the name.

"The preservation of the stained glass windows will always be an ongoing project," he said. "That window was threatened because it needed so much work. To be honest, I think some in the church consider it an inappropriate image to have above the altar." He smiled. "But I quite like it. Ties us to the past and let's say, the exotic beginnings of our faith. Reminds us to remember the Middle East in our prayers."

Morgan wanted to encourage his friendliness but they didn't have much time.

"It was threatened, you say …?"

"Yes, but then there was a large donation, specifically tied to that window."

"Do you have any records of the details, or anything that was left behind along with the donation?"

The old man rubbed his chin. "Hmm, let me see. I'll have to go out back but you've piqued my interest, young lady. Why don't you wait in the Chapter House and I'll come find you when I've had a look."

Morgan didn't see that they had any choice. She nodded. "Thank you, I really appreciate your help."

She and Jake walked back down the cloisters towards the Chapter House.

"The world turns on the curiosity of one man," Jake whispered. "But I'm glad we don't have to break in here and look for it ourselves."

"That's if he finds anything."

They walked into the octagonal Chapter House, bright with sunlight that poured in through high windows. A decorative medieval frieze circled the interior above the stalls, alive with figures from Genesis and Exodus. Morgan recognized Adam and Eve, Abraham, Noah and even the Tower of Babel. A gigantic display case dominated one side. A group of tourists huddled around it as their guide explained the manuscript within.

"This is one of the four surviving original copies of the Magna Carta, the Great Charter or peace treaty that promised protections against a tyrannical King."

The guide continued to explain the history of the document but Morgan tuned out her words. She looked at her watch. Time ticked on. She imagined the old man rifling through boxes in a long hall of records. Would he even find anything?

The sound of footsteps came from the corridor and then the old man emerged.

"I found this." He held up a small rectangular package wrapped in brown paper, dusty from the storeroom. It had her name written clearly on the front in thick black ink. "Are you Morgan Sierra?"

Morgan pulled out her driver's license. He looked at it, nodded and then handed her the box.

"I'll just go and photocopy this for the records," he said. "Back in a minute."

The tourist group walked out of the Chapter House and they were alone.

"I'm not waiting any longer."

Morgan crouched down on the floor and peeled open the package. Inside was a plain cedar-wood box. There were no carvings as would be expected from a Dominican friar. Morgan smiled. Ben was never one for over-decoration or fussiness.

She opened it.

CHAPTER 25

INSIDE THE BOX WAS a note and another package, wrapped tight in oilskin. Morgan opened the note first. Ben's spidery handwriting stood out on the cream paper.

My dearest Morgan,

If you nd this, I m gone and I m sorry to leave you with this burden. I found this vial with the seal in Ephesus. The carvings in the tomb where I discovered it referenced a serpent trapped for a thousand years and suggested that this was some kind of antidote or weapon. I don t know which, or what it s for. But I know enough of evil to trust how important this is. Whether the serpent is real or alle-gorical, this may help in the ght against it.

May God guide you and give you His strength,

Ben

Morgan unwrapped the package.

It contained a vial made of thick glass, tightly sealed with creamy wax. The glass was opaque but the color within was a deep scarlet.

"Blood?" Jake suggested.

"Could be." Morgan held it up to the light. The liquid inside was viscous and stuck to the sides as she swirled it. "I should get this to Martin to test in the labs, right?"

Jake nodded. "That would be the best plan."

"But Ben said specifically to keep it away from ARKANE …"

"And given what happened to Martin," Jake continued, "it might not be safe to take the vial into HQ right now."

Morgan nodded. "So we keep it with us until this is done."

Her phone buzzed with a message from Martin.

The confluence of the stars is imminent and the eclipse will cover Jerusalem tomorrow. We've had reports of a sarcophagus being taken into the Old City of Jerusalem by night. Flights booked out of Heathrow for you both.

Jake checked his phone for the details. "Looks like we need to get going."

Morgan slipped the vial into her backpack. "Let's finish this."

* * *

Jerusalem, Israel.

Deep underneath the citadel, the sound of dripping water echoed through the tunnel. Then came heavy breathing from the men who hauled the massive stone sarcophagus towards the central chamber.

"Careful!" Cardinal Eric Krotalia shouted as it bumped the walls, leaving a chip off the stone. But he could do nothing to widen the tight tunnel and he waved the men on, standing back as they continued down.

He wiped the sweat from his brow, more from anxiety than physical exertion, since Samael's men were the ones doing all the work. Samael himself was at the head of the group, directing the sacred object towards the chamber. His man Krait heaved at his side, and the woman he had brought, Lilith, slid sinuously ahead of them. She wore a green silk robe, hood covering her face, but he thought he glimpsed scales on her skin and a flash of green eyes in the torchlight.

Truth be told, he was nervous about bringing the sarcophagus down here. Somehow it suddenly made everything real. The ancient Brotherhood of the Serpent had survived as a secret organization for longer than history recorded, perhaps unbroken since the times of ancient Egypt, when Moses raised his brazen serpent in the desert. As much as the Cardinal believed the apocalyptic rhetoric, he had not seriously believed that he would be part of the End of Days.

Until he had seen the markings on the sarcophagus earlier.

Now it was here and doubts crept in. He didn't know what would happen when it was opened. What if he couldn't control the following events? His plans were for an earthly battle, the positioning of pawns on the chessboard of military strategy, enhanced by religious conflict. A changing of the guard in the Middle East, where it was time for Christianity to take a stronger role again, as it had in the Middle Ages. It was likely that Cerastes and Echis thought exactly the same thing: that they would be the ones to triumph once the status quo was gone. But what if none of them were able to contain whatever was in here?

The Cardinal sighed and pressed his hand against the cold stone of the tunnel wall, letting the physical sensation anchor him to what was real. It was all superstitious nonsense. The Great Serpent was allegory. There would be nothing but dust in the chest.

But he had to make sure.

He had promised to wait until Cerastes and Echis arrived before opening it, but he needed to know what they were dealing with.

They finally rolled the sarcophagus into the cistern and Samael dismissed the men, sending them back up to the Old City with enough money to keep their mouths shut. He indicated Krait should stay.

After the footsteps and coarse laughter faded into silence, only four of them stood in the chamber looking at the sarcophagus.

"Do you have the seals?" the Cardinal asked.

Samael put down his pack and opened it up. He pulled out each stone seal in turn and placed them on the floor in front of him.

"There. Seven in total."

Lilith knelt by the seals, her fingers reaching out to touch them. The Cardinal bent to pull her away.

"Don't touch them! You're not worthy."

As he yanked back her shoulder, she turned her face up. The hood fell away. She hissed at him, sibilance echoing in the chamber.

The Cardinal gasped, his hand flying to his mouth in shock. The woman's face was skeletal thin, her green eyes slitted and glazed, her tongue forked as it flickered towards him.

Samael put his hand on her shoulder. His eyes met the Cardinal's, warning him away.

"It's alright, Lilith. The Cardinal was just trying to honor the Great Serpent. He didn't realize how close you are to Him. How well you have taken to the venom."

"I …"

The Cardinal didn't know what to say, but if this was

what the venom could do, then he was glad he hadn't taken it himself. He straightened his robe and took a deep breath. "Well then, perhaps we should take a look inside."

"Yesss. It is time." Lilith's voice made the Cardinal shiver, as if it called to something base inside, the part of him that descended from a common vertebral ancestor.

He glanced over at Krait.

Samael saw his look. "Oh, you can trust Krait, and he deserves to be here."

The Cardinal nodded. Part of him wanted to be one who opened the casket, but he couldn't risk himself. Let Samael take the chance. "Proceed."

Samael picked up the first seal and pressed it to the sarcophagus on top of the indent matching the seal's markings. His fingers shook a little as he slotted it into the ancient stone.

Nothing happened.

"Do the next one!" the Cardinal ordered.

Lilith handed Samael the next seal and once again, he pushed it into the waiting space. Nothing.

Impatient now, he quickly added the next and Lilith joined him, adding the others until all seven were tucked into their spaces on the edge of the sarcophagus.

The Cardinal held his breath, waiting for something … He didn't know what. But all this effort couldn't have been for nothing. His heart sank as he considered possible failure.

Then something inside the stone casket clunked.

A crack appeared along the side.

The sound of thunder rolled through the cistern as if a storm crashed directly overhead. The great pillars cracked and chunks of masonry fell from above. The Cardinal fell to his knees, protecting his head with his arms. Lilith cried out in an exclamation of excitement.

The top of the sarcophagus creaked open. Just a crack, but it was enough.

Samael turned to Krait. "A crowbar, quick."

Krait grabbed one from the corner of the room. Together, they wedged the end into the crack and began to lever the heavy lid up and away from the side, managing to push it up an inch further.

A salty musk of decomposition rose from the opening. Both men recoiled, hands clutched to their faces in disgust. The Cardinal coughed and tried to swallow down the retching that threatened to overwhelm him.

Something had died in there. A long time ago.

But Lilith bent to the crack. She put her face close to it, inhaling the noxious smell as if it were roses, her face contorted in ecstasy. What the hell did she sense that he couldn't?

"Pusssh it further." Her eyes glinted with excitement. "So we can see inside."

Samael wedged the crowbar back into the gap and between them, he and Krait managed to lever the lid even further, sliding it back until it crashed on the floor behind the open casket.

Lilith was the first to look at what lay inside. Her hands flew to her mouth in shock.

"No!" she cried.

The Cardinal stepped forward to stand next to the sarcophagus, Samael and Krait next to him. He looked within.

It was half-filled with grey-green dust, like a powdered form of algae. A deep disappointment filled his body, along with a rising anger.

Samael pushed the end of the crowbar into the dust, raking it around a little just to check if anything was beneath. There was nothing. He turned to Lilith.

"I guess you were wrong."

Her eyes flashed with anger. She wrenched her hand back, putting all her weight into slapping him across the face.

Her serpent ring caught his lip and a drop of blood flew from his mouth to land in the green dust.

"You bitch –" Sam's words stopped abruptly as he saw the blood droplet soaking up the green powder. It changed, hardening and shimmering in the torchlight until it was a perfectly formed bright green polygon.

The Cardinal bent to pick it up and held it to the light.

"Is that what I think it is?" Samael said softly.

The Cardinal nodded. "It's a scale."

Lilith plucked it from his fingers. "We need more blood."

CHAPTER 26

THE CARDINAL BACKED AWAY from the sarcophagus, retreating to the corner of the cistern. Sam met Lilith's gaze, understanding flashing between them.

He spun around with the crowbar, smashing it into Krait's face.

The man flew backwards, stunned at the sudden attack, clutching his broken face as he moaned in pain. Sam whirled the crowbar round again, whacking Krait in the kneecap. The man went down, roaring in pain. Sam raised the weapon to swing the final blow.

Krait surged up from the floor, like an angry bull charging for its life.

He smashed Sam into the side of the sarcophagus. Sam doubled over as the air was driven out of him.

The crowbar fell clattering to the floor. Krait's hands found Sam's neck and squeezed, even as the blood from his injuries dripped down onto the floor.

"You bastard," Krait grunted. "After everything I've done for you and the Brotherhood."

As the edges of his vision began to fade, Sam saw Lilith pick up the crowbar. She swung it at the back of Krait's head.

It connected with a sickening thunk. Krait's hands dropped away and he spun to face the new attacker. It looked like the blow had done nothing but anger him further. Sam fell to his knees, choking on the floor, trying desperately to catch his breath.

Lilith backed away, her hands raised in supplication.

Krait advanced on her. "It's about time you …"

His words trailed off as he faltered. His hands clutched at his head, and then he slumped unconscious to the floor.

Lilith rushed to the fallen man. She grabbed his hands and pulled him back towards the casket.

"Help me! He won't be out for long."

Sam stumbled to his feet and helped lift Krait's body. Together they heaved him over the edge and into the sarcophagus. He thumped down into the grey-green dust, some of it rising to hang in the air around him.

Lilith pulled a knife from her belt. Her green eyes glinted with black slits again, and Sam wondered once more who she had become. She pulled back on Krait's hair with one hand, exposing his throat.

Then she plunged the knife down and tugged it towards her, slitting his jugular vein.

Blood gushed from the wound, pumping out on to the dust. It began to transform into scales that drew themselves together, coalescing into clumps, then tiny worm-like creatures. They wriggled over Krait's body, dissolving his skin and slipping inside, becoming part of him. Eating his body from the inside out. It was mesmerizing to watch.

Suddenly, Krait's eyes flew open in agony.

He tried to sit up, gurgling through the bloody wound at his throat. Sam and Lilith pushed him back, holding him down in the dust as he became a writhing, pulsating mass of bloody flesh.

The Cardinal joined them at the edge of the sarcophagus once it was clear that Krait was really dead. They stood in silence as the body was consumed. By the time it was done, a long chain of scaly lumps lay writhing on the top of the grey-green dust. It wasn't a serpent yet, but Sam could see the beginnings of what it might become. He could feel a twinge of excitement in his belly. This mess of half-formed thing was nothing, but there was still a great deal of grey-green dust remaining.

Lilith still held the bloody knife. She turned towards Sam and the Cardinal. "None of us go in there. Agreed?"

The Cardinal nodded. "Of course. There are plenty more we can find to pay the blood price." He looked down at the writhing mass. "How many do we need?"

A smile played across Lilith's lips and she flickered her forked tongue in the air as if tasting the sacrifice to come. "Ssseven is the sacred number."

Sam had plenty of contacts on the darker side of the city. He looked at his watch. "Give me a couple of hours."

The Cardinal nodded. "Hurry. The confluence of stars and the full moon eclipse coincide at 9:33 p.m., when Jerusalem will be in darkness. My brothers will be here and together, we will greet the Great Serpent."

* * *

Morgan and Jake got out of the taxi at the Damascus Gate. Originally built as a triumphal entrance in Roman times, the existing sixteenth-century gate had been built by the Ottoman Sultan, Suleiman the Magnificent. It was hot and noisy since the ancient place was right next to a busy bus station and highway intersection. Jerusalem had ever been a vibrant city, concerned more with the living than the empires of the dead. Tourist groups headed into the city following guides with colorful umbrellas, while locals expertly dodged those taking photos.

Jake finished paying the taxi driver.

"Martin said that a sarcophagus arrived last night as part of a shipment for Hebrew University but it never arrived. It was diverted to a residential area in the Jewish Quarter of the Old City."

"We'll head that way then," Morgan said. "Through the Arab souk."

They walked together under the arch. The Old City walls towered above them and Morgan felt a renewed respect for the city she had grown up with. It seemed she only came back here at times of crisis these days. When she did, the longing to stay welled up within her. But there were so many ghosts of her past here, Elian and her father, old friends who had moved on. She had another life now.

The narrow streets of the bazaar bustled with people. Tourist shops catered to all religions here, some stalls selling Jewish *yarmulke* alongside olive wood crucifixes and gilt plates inscribed with Arabic calligraphy. The smell of falafel wafted from one tiny shop, the fried chickpea balls with salad in pita bread a Jerusalem favorite.

Old men sat outside their shops drinking tiny cups of thick black Arab coffee, flavored with cardamom. Women in hijab haggled over the price of vegetables while the sound of the muezzin drowned the noise of the market in the call to prayer. As they walked past the Stations of the Cross, a group of Christian pilgrims chanted as they carried a life-size wooden cross on the route Christ himself had walked.

At the edge of the Jewish Quarter, Morgan stopped at a fruit stall piled high with light green melon and brilliant red pomegranates. Plastic cups filled with chopped pieces of juicy fruit stood at the front of the stall. She paid a few shekels to the vendor and picked two up. For a moment, she and Jake just stood on the edge of the market relishing the diversity of the city, enjoying sweetness after a long journey.

The sun warmed Morgan's face and the sounds of the souk swirled around them. Morgan tried to embrace the moment. Even without Ben in her life anymore, she had her family. She had Jake. Yet she was walking into danger once again, and her anger had driven her here. It was hubris to think that they could somehow stop the End of Days. This city was threatened daily by destruction, but it had continued to survive for thousands of years. Fruit sellers had sold to weary travelers since the earliest days in this very spot. Romans, Crusaders, Ottomans, Jews. They would continue after she and Jake were long gone.

Morgan took a final bite.

"Right, let's find this sarcophagus."

They ducked through an ornate arch and emerged into a square. Morgan looked towards the golden Dome of the Rock on Temple Mount before them, a sense of foreboding rising within her.

"Parts of the Jewish Quarter are awfully close to the boundary. I wonder …" Her words trailed off as she stared up. "There are rumors of tunnels underneath the Temple Mount. Excavation isn't allowed, of course."

"But what if there was a way to get underneath?" Jake shook his head. "This would be the perfect place to kick off the End of Days."

Morgan pulled out her phone and called Martin.

"Can you scan through the plans for this area of Jerusalem? I want to know who owns the buildings, particularly the ones closer to the edge of the Temple Mount."

"Give me ten minutes."

Morgan turned to Jake. "Let's keep walking. We might find something."

The white stone reflected the heat of the sun, keeping the interiors cooler. There were no gardens in this densely packed neighborhood but flower boxes bloomed in little windows, a glimmer of color against the pale walls. There were *mezuzahs* on the doorposts, little decorative boxes containing parchment inscribed with specific verses from the Torah, the prayer of Shema Yisrael.

Hear, O Israel, the Lord our God, the Lord is one.

Morgan remembered the *mezuzah* by her father's door in Safed, decorated with the sacred blue of Kabbalah. Israel had taken so much from her, but its intensity was the bedrock of her life. Maybe the ghosts were not those of the dead who remained here now, an echo in the olive groves and ancient ruins. Maybe she was the ghost. Flitting around from country to country, living on the edge for the mission and leaving a piece of her soul behind every time.

A buzz on her phone.

"I think I've found it." Martin stumbled over the words. "It has to be him, it has to be that man, that –"

"Slow down, tell me what you've found."

"There's a Vatican retreat house a few streets from where you are now. Three years ago, plans for interior modification were filed with the Jerusalem council. The name on the application was Eric Krotalia."

"The Cardinal?"

"The very same."

"Send through the details and we'll head over there now."

* * *

This time he would make sure everything would be done properly and with ceremony, as befitted the momentous occasion. The Cardinal lit the final candle and looked around in satisfaction. Golden light flickered in the corners of the stone vault, dancing over the open sarcophagus and its writhing inhabitant. He shivered a little, and he knew it wasn't the cold.

Thoughts of the Great Serpent had filled his mind since he was a boy in the hills of rural Greece. As a young orphan he had been taken in by the local monastery and it was there he had started his rise within the Church. He had been recruited as a young priest into the Brotherhood, drawn to them by the promise of a rapid ascent through the layers of ecclesiastical hierarchy. And now he stood at the crux of history and yet …

He walked to the open sarcophagus and looked down at the pathetic creature within. It was just a big lump of green and grey flesh, writhing with some kind of life force imbued by the death of the first man, Krait. It was base and gross. The Cardinal shook his head and exhaled slowly. Where was the majesty? Where was the terror?

What would Cerastes and Echis think when they arrived? Had they really sent the world into turmoil for this?

He turned away, disgusted at his own lack of faith, but he couldn't look at the thing any longer. He could only hope that Samael brought enough bodies to turn it into something worthy of his allegiance.

The sound of singing came from the corner of the room. Lilith sat on the ground, painting her skin with swirls like the undulations of the serpent. He had forgotten she was even there. She looked up at him, her green eyes flickering.

"You doubt, Cardinal. He knows thisss."

Her smile was predatory and he wondered again at her sanity, but he also felt a white-hot jealousy at her seeming trust in the serpent. He made up his mind. He would take the venom at the time of sacrifice. He would join her in her deep faith as the Great Serpent was resurrected.

There was a scuffle of footsteps in the tunnel. Samael walked in with a group of men, each carrying a body wrapped in a shroud over their shoulders. The men laid their burdens down in front of the sarcophagus and retreated back up the tunnel, hurrying away with the haste of those fleeing certain death.

As Samael began to unwrap the first body, two figures emerged from the shadows across the cistern. Cerastes and Echis.

"Welcome, brothers." The Cardinal's confident smile returned. "You're just in time to witness the resurrection."

CHAPTER 27

THE ECLIPSE WAS ALMOST at its zenith as Morgan and Jake reached the house that Martin had identified. The darkness was nearly complete and the sky was a dull rust.

"The sun will be turned to darkness and the moon to blood before the coming of the great and dreadful day of the Lord." Morgan looked at Jake. "The book of Joel, chapter two."

"Or, it could just be a lunar eclipse," Jake said. "The earth's shadow on the moon's face appears dark until it covers the moon entirely and then it looks red. The earth's atmosphere changes the light spectrum, filtering out the green to violet, leaving only the red behind."

Morgan smiled and punched his arm. "Where's your sense of occasion?"

Suddenly, the door of the house slammed open. A group of men darted out, eyes wide with panic. They ran off down the road as if demons chased them.

"What the –?"

Morgan was already running for the door they had left wide open behind them.

"Come on, we have to find what they were running from."

They ran into the house and found another door open in the kitchen. A stone staircase led downward, lit by weak lights. A metallic smell of blood and the stench of decay emanated from beyond.

"This must lead under the Temple Mount," Morgan whispered.

Jake nodded. "And by that smell, I'd say they've started without us. Let's get going."

Together, they descended the steps, careful to walk as quietly as they could.

Morgan heard chanting as they reached the bottom of the staircase. She peeked around the corner to see a vault hollowed out of an ancient stone cistern. A group of people stood around a stone sarcophagus watching something inside. Four bodies lay on the ground next to them.

Something lifted out from the sarcophagus.

A green curve of a snake's coil, its body as thick as her own waist.

* * *

Lilith watched as Samael lifted the next body and heaved it into the sarcophagus. A young Arab, his muscles honed from manual labor. She nodded her head in approval at his choice. The man's strength was worthy for the offering.

She bent with the knife and sliced his throat. Bright blood gushed out over the coils of the serpent, bathing it in gore. She felt the other men's eyes on her, and understood they feared her in some way. But she no longer cared for their opinion. She only had eyes for the serpent.

It shuddered with a kind of ecstasy as it consumed the sacrifice and began to pulsate as it grew yet again. She reached out with one hand and stroked its skin. The green scales were iridescent and variegated, like the feathers of a tropical bird, like emeralds at the heart of the earth. They were cool and hard, almost metallic to her touch but underneath, she could feel the pulse of its blood.

She could hear His voice more clearly now. The last of

the venom was gone, coursing through her veins but Lilith knew she wouldn't need it again. Now she would commune with Him directly. Her entire life had led her to this moment, to this encounter, and she vibrated with the energy of His resurrection. She thought back to the church where she had first held snakes, her misdirected belief that it was God who wanted her to take hold of them. When really, it had been the Serpent of Serpents, calling her to His side.

Now she was here. Now she was ready.

Echis looked at his watch.

"We have to hurry, the eclipse is at its zenith."

The Cardinal glanced at the remaining bodies. "If we each lift one, we can finish this."

He dragged one of the bodies to the other side of the sarcophagus, pulling the man's neck to the edge. Echis took another and Samael helped the old man, Cerastes. They held the final three offerings on the lip of the stone casket.

Lilith cut each neck in turn, each slash making her sigh with pleasure. The blood rained down on the serpent. It writhed in the gore, bathing itself, coating its scales as it absorbed the fluid and flesh. They pushed the bodies in.

The coils started to grow faster.

The sarcophagus creaked and cracked as the serpent's muscular body pushed against the boundaries of the casket. Lilith stepped back as she realized what was about to happen. He could not be contained any longer.

A loud crack resounded in the cistern.

The serpent exploded from the sarcophagus. As the stone fragmented, its coils tumbled from the prison it had been held in for a thousand years.

Lilith felt His exultation at being free. He reared up even as He grew even faster, His massive head turning towards the men below. His eyes were hard emeralds, a shifting intelligence behind an animal physicality.

The Cardinal fell to his knees in front of the serpent, his

hands lifted in supplication. "Great Serpent, we serve –"

The snake reared back and struck with lighting speed, its fangs like swords piercing straight through the Cardinal's body. His words broke off, his eyes widening in horror as he died.

Echis darted towards the tunnel but the serpent swung its gigantic tail, knocking the man off his feet and crushing him beneath the writhing coils even as it absorbed the Cardinal's flesh.

Cerastes stood like a statue, his old frame shaking a little. He smiled, almost with resignation, his eyes wide at the glorious, terrible sight.

"The thousand years are ended!" he shouted in triumph. The serpent wrapped its coils around him, crushing the air from his lungs and absorbing the man within its ever-growing form.

Samael darted behind a pillar, crushing himself as far into a corner as he could, making himself small so as not to catch the snake's attention. Lilith could smell his fear even from this distance. These pitiful men. They should have understood that they were only here to be consumed. He needed their blood for His power.

Come to me.

She heard Him speak as He had through the venom, but now He was here. Lilith's heart pounded in her chest as she stepped forward in front of the Great Serpent, offering herself to Him. His giant head swung around, His eyes fixed upon her. She thought she saw recognition there. Her blood was mostly venom now, her body already transforming into a serpent.

This was her fate.

In a flash, the massive serpent whipped its coils around her and crushed her body to Him. Lilith heard her bones snap as she was broken apart, but the pain was part of another life. The venom took her mind above the agony and she relaxed into His embrace, releasing the air from her lungs as He crushed her ever closer.

She felt a burning, melting sensation and her skin began to morph and ripple as she was absorbed. The snake pulsated around her and she became a part of it, fusing with its flesh.

In the last moments, her awareness spread, separating from the pain. She was no longer an empty bag of flesh and bones, no longer a frail woman. She was in the serpent. She was part of Him. She could feel the undulations of His thick musculature, the slip of cool stone underneath. She could sense the vibrations of others nearby.

Above and around, out there in the city, there were so many more.

With every sacrifice, she would grow stronger and bigger, more powerful. The city waited. But first ...

The serpent turned back towards the corner where Samael cowered.

* * *

Morgan watched in horror as Lilith was crushed and twisted and then somehow, became a part of the Great Serpent. It grew as her body was absorbed into its skin and suddenly, there seemed an all-too-human glint in its eyes, a female intelligence.

Its giant head whipped around and stared at Samael cowering in the corner. His face contorted in terror as it slithered across the cistern floor.

"I am your servant." His hands pushed at the coils of flesh as they pushed against him. "Lilith. No!"

Morgan watched the snake toy with him a little, its head swaying hypnotically. Then it reared back to strike.

Samael had killed Ben. He had left them to die in Egypt. Morgan felt nothing as the serpent's head darted forward, its gigantic fangs slicing down. Samael's scream echoed in the chamber as he was pierced, crushed and consumed.

But the serpent would not be occupied for long with Samael's meager body. It would soon want more. Its coils were almost at two meters thick now, hugely powerful, growing with every sacrifice it absorbed.

"We need to leave," Jake said, heading up a few stairs. "Get a military strike team down here and blow this freak of nature to bits."

"It's too late." Morgan watched as the snake grew even larger. "It will burst out of the cistern soon. The Temple Mount is above us, the Western Wall is so close. Who knows what power this thing will have once it gets too big and escapes into the city. We have to stop it down here." She stepped out of the tunnel into the cistern.

"No, Morgan." Jake ran back down and grabbed her arm, but she tugged out of his grip.

This was her city.

She could not let this unholy thing destroy the sacred places around them. It would spark a religious war not seen here since the time of the Crusades. Blood would run in the alleyways of Jerusalem again and she would not allow it.

She took another step into the chamber. The Great Serpent swung its head around, blood dripping from its fangs. It fixed its eyes upon her.

CHAPTER 28

THE GREAT SERPENT HISSED and undulated across the stone floor towards Morgan. It grew with every breath, its body expanding with thick muscle and shimmering dark magic. It was magnificent now, with a strange and terrible grace. Its emerald green eyes sparkled in the candlelight and Morgan was hypnotized by the stark beauty of it. Lucifer was said to have been the most beautiful of the angels. Was that dark presence in this creature now? Was anything left of those it had consumed?

Then she remembered the vial that Ben had found with the seal. Perhaps those ancient protectors had known this day would come.

"The vial, Jake. Quickly!"

Morgan feinted in one direction as the snake's giant body slid through the blood left from the sacrifice. Its mouth opened wide, its fangs dripping venom onto the stone where it bubbled as it dissolved the cistern beneath it.

It reared back and darted forward.

Morgan commando-rolled away. She felt the rush of air against the back of her neck as the snake barely missed her. She rose to her feet again, glancing over to see Jake rummaging through the pack for the vial.

"Now would be good." She ran around the perimeter of the cistern and ducked behind what remained of one of the gigantic pillars.

The serpent curled around, forked tongue flickering as it tasted the air. Then she felt a presence in her mind, pushing into her brain.

Become part of me and you will see eternity. Jussst rest now.

Morgan shook her head, trying to wrestle the voice away but it persisted, echoing through her mind, offering her the world if she would just let it consume her.

But she knew this foe.

He was the persuader. The liar. The whisper that convinced Eve to eat the fruit of forbidden knowledge. He would be the End of Days, consuming all that was good in creation. But he was also seduction and some part of her wanted to let him take her, to end her last breath here beneath the ancient Holy of Holies. She was so tired.

"I've got it," Jake called, breaking the spell. He eased out of the tunnel, holding the vial aloft in his hand. He met Morgan's eyes across the stone chamber.

But the Great Serpent blocked the path between them. Its head whipped around to look at Jake, then it spun and lunged forward towards Morgan.

She darted left but the serpent's coils slammed into the sarcophagus in front of her, smashing what was left of it into tiny pieces. She zigzagged away but there was nowhere left to go.

She was trapped. It would be upon her in a second.

"Throw it!" She held her hands up as the serpent coiled around her lower body.

Its first embrace was firm but not tight, the pressure like being rolled in a blanket. Immovable and yet somehow comforting.

Then she felt a burning sensation on her legs and gasped. It didn't want to crush her, but it was dissolving her somehow, consuming her straight into its flesh.

While its tail end held Morgan tight, the serpent pursued

Jake as he tried to get to her across the room. It was like a stone obstacle course, but he kept coming, darting between pillars, leaping over broken masonry.

Then he tripped.

His eyes widened. The snake's head darted in, fangs bared.

In that moment, Jake threw the vial. He rolled to the floor behind the remains of the sarcophagus as the snake bit down into his flesh.

Morgan reached up and caught the vial in the zenith of its arc. What was it for? Should she drink it? Inject it into the snake somehow? She searched desperately for an answer even as she heard Jake's scream of agony.

Her friend was dying. There was no time left.

The scientist in her understood that the serpent must have some kind of membrane on its skin to dissolve and consume flesh that way. As the burning intensified in her legs, she could only think of one thing to do.

She pulled the top from the vial and poured it between their flesh into the space where its coils consumed her lower body. She wrapped her arms around it and hugged it closer to her, willing the liquid to work.

The snake's head whipped up, its fangs bloody. It let out a high-pitched squeal of pain. It shook its coils, unraveling from Morgan, trying to shake her off.

But she held on.

She pressed her body onto it, keeping the liquid from the vial between them, forcing it onto the serpent's flesh. It was a cool balm to her, softening the flames that burned her lower limbs but the snake thrashed as if it were the fires of Hell itself. She just needed to hold on …

The serpent reared up on its powerful tail and thrashed in the air, shaking its body as it tried to escape the burning. Morgan spun out of its grip and smashed into the stone wall of the cistern, her body broken and bruised.

The serpent screamed, a sound that came from the depths of the pit, a bubbling, drowning screech accompanied by the stench of rotting flesh from the depths of the ocean. Morgan looked up to see a deep wound opening up on its side, like a flesh-eating disease that consumed it even as it continued to grow.

The serpent thrashed and twisted. In its need to escape the pain, it smashed into the great wall of the cistern. It hurled itself against the stone, breaking it apart, and tunneled away, screaming, up towards the Western Wall.

Morgan laid her head down on the cool stone beneath her, eyes fixed on Jake lying prone by the sarcophagus, his body a mass of blood. The pain of bubbling fire burned her legs and she dared not look down at them. But the serpent was wounded and she could only hope that it would die before it laid waste to the city above.

She and Jake could do no more.

* * *

As the sun went dark under the full eclipse, crowds gathered at the Western Wall to pray for deliverance. Men in their shawls and curls, women in modest dresses. Children ran around playing, unaware of the devastation that had been foreseen in ancient times.

The giant stones at the bottom of the Wall suddenly exploded out with the force of the great creature beneath.

Shards of rock splintered away, raining down on those close by. Screams erupted in the plaza and people ran for the streets beyond as the Great Serpent emerged into the square.

It thrashed its gigantic tail, propelling it forward, shaking its head as it tried to escape the agony of the burning. It crushed those in its path, wrapping its coils around any it could catch, trying to subsume their corpses even as it plunged its fangs into more bodies. But the wound ate away at its flesh faster than it could replace it with fresh blood.

The serpent screamed in agony, rising up on its coils to tower above the square, daring these mortals to challenge it.

But this was not the Israel of thousands of years ago.

Israeli soldiers stationed permanently in the square opened fire from all sides. International police on the Temple Mount shot down from on high. A military helicopter darted in overhead, soldiers peppering the serpent with bullets from above.

The Great Serpent felt the sting of the bullets, fighting to repair its wounds, but it weakened as the burning in its flank spread, the hole growing.

It fell to the ground, writhing in agony as it succumbed to the overwhelming force of destruction. Gunfire tore apart what was left until only chunks of flesh remained. Soon only piles of grey-green dust lay in the square, clouds of it blowing away, scattered by the wind.

The military moved in to take control of the scene. A group of soldiers approached the massive hole in the Western Wall, aiming flashlights down into the depths.

"Get the medics," one shouted. "There's people down here."

CHAPTER 29

Oxford, England. A week later.

MORGAN WATCHED AS THE coffin was lowered into
the ground of the Catholic graveyard. This would be Ben's
last resting place and one he would appreciate because he
loved this city. Not that Ben was in there. Morgan looked up
at the grey sky into the falling drops of rain. She didn't know
what happened after death, but Ben had been a man of faith
so she hoped he was with the God he'd served for a lifetime.

Even after death, he had saved her life one more time.
The contents of the vial had wounded the serpent enough
that the military were able to finish it off. The press was still
on fire with speculation about what had happened. Amateur
footage of the serpent bursting through the Western Wall
shook the international news headlines. Some called it a
relic of the dinosaur era that had somehow slept under the
Temple Mount. Others called it the Great Serpent from the
pit in Revelation heralding the beginning of the End Times.

Whatever they said, it was gone now but Morgan knew
the threats weren't over. The news would always be filled
with the next crisis. Such was the drama of human life. But
perhaps she didn't have to take part in the next chapter.

She used her new walking stick to hobble around the
grave and back to the path. Jake joined her but he didn't try
to take her arm and help. Morgan appreciated his respect

for her independence. She was getting treatment for the unusual chemical burns that lacerated her legs but pain still lanced through her every day. Jake had deep wounds from the fangs that pierced his flesh that night, but he had recovered quickly. Whatever had happened in New York had given him some kind of healing ability. Morgan wished she could have some of it. She wanted to run again, she needed to move, but her wounds kept her at this slow pace.

Together they walked slowly back through the city to the Museum of Natural History. They entered the Pitt Rivers Museum and descended into the ARKANE labs beneath the city. Morgan remembered the first night she had come here, when Jake was still a stranger, when she knew nothing of ARKANE. Her family were safe and back home now, so she had come full circle. Perhaps that was as it should be.

They walked into one of the labs. Director Marietti stood up from one of the desks and came over to greet them both.

"I'm so sorry, Morgan. I know Ben meant a lot to you."

Morgan nodded. Marietti shook hands with Jake.

"You did a great job stopping the serpent, and I hope you're ready for a new mission." Marietti turned and brought up the details on screen. "A body has been found in New Orleans, covered in occult markings. It's not the first. ARKANE New York have sent agent Naomi Locasto down there. I know you've worked with her before, Jake, when you were in New York, and I think you'll work well with her too, Morgan."

Morgan took a deep breath. She was suddenly sure of what she needed to do. "I'm not going."

Jake spun around to face her. She saw the hurt in his eyes, but no surprise.

"I'm done for now. I need time to think, time with my family."

Marietti nodded. "Of course." He paused. "But we'll need to rescind your security access. I'll have Martin process your exit."

His words were so clinical, so final. Morgan hesitated. She could still stay, still change her mind. She could be part of the next mission with Jake. They could still be a team. She looked up at the screen. It would be a fascinating case.

But not for her.

Marietti put out his hand. "We'll miss you, Morgan. The door is always open for you to return."

Morgan took his hand and shook it, feeling the reassuring strength in his grip. "Goodbye, sir."

* * *

Jake walked out of the door with her, saying nothing as they headed towards the exit, but his mind was in turmoil. He couldn't let her go. As they turned the corner, out of hearing range from the lab, Morgan stopped him.

"I'm so sorry. I just can't keep doing this." She placed a hand on his arm. "I've put my family at risk, and Ben ..." A tear ran down her cheek. "I might as well have killed him myself."

"Don't say that." Jake pulled her to him, enfolding her in his arms. "Ben wouldn't have wanted you to blame yourself."

She laid her head against his chest and he stroked her hair, trying to soothe the tears that came freely now.

"Please don't ask me to stay, Jake." She pulled back a little and looked up at him. Her blue eyes glistened with tears and the violet slash burned with intensity. "I need time to think about whether this can work. Whether I can work for ARKANE again."

Jake saw the conflict in her eyes and he understood why she felt so torn. He had no family left to risk, and the years as an agent had made him more independent, separated from those around him. Morgan was the closest he had to a friend, Director Marietti and Martin were his family. ARKANE was his stability. When he thought about a separate life, of giving up being an agent, he found he couldn't even consider another option. This life defined him. But Morgan had other options and other people she loved.

He was not her world.

"I understand," he said quietly. He pulled her close again and kissed her forehead gently. "I'll miss you so much."

Jake knew he would go to America and join Naomi Locasto in New Orleans. He could only hope that Morgan would be here when he returned.

* * *

The adventures continue for the
ARKANE team in *Valley of Dry Bones,* available now.

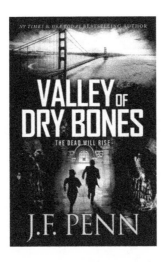

An ancient prophecy. An occult secret.
The power to raise the dead.

When a long-hidden tomb and a body covered in Voodoo symbols are found in New Orleans, ARKANE agent Jake Timber discovers a mystery that stretches back to the Spanish Empire and the bloody dungeons of the Inquisition.

But he is not the only one who seeks the Hand of Ezekiel.

A shadowy billionaire, backed by those who seek immortality at any price, will stop at nothing to find the relics that can turn bones to living flesh.

When disaster strikes in the heart of the Louisiana bayou, Jake calls on ARKANE agent Morgan Sierra to help him once more as they race against time across the outposts of the Spanish Empire.

From Madrid and Toledo to the Philippines, Peru, and on to New Orleans and San Francisco, can Morgan and Jake find the relics and stop the resurrection of the dead?

ENJOYED END OF DAYS?

If you loved the book and have a moment to spare, I would really appreciate a short review on the page where you bought the book. Your help in spreading the word is gratefully appreciated and reviews make a huge difference to helping new readers find the series. Thank you!

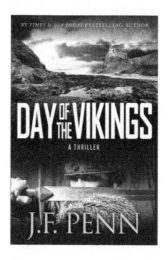

Get a free copy of the bestselling thriller, *Day of the Vikings*, ARKANE book 5, when you sign up to join my Reader's Group. You'll also be notified of new releases, giveaways and receive personal updates from behind the scenes of my thrillers.

WWW.JFPENN.COM/FREE

* * *

Day of the Vikings, an ARKANE thriller

A ritual murder on a remote island under the shifting skies of the aurora borealis.

A staff of power that can summon Ragnarok, the Viking apocalypse.

When Neo-Viking terrorists invade the British Museum in London to reclaim the staff of Skara Brae, ARKANE agent Dr. Morgan Sierra is trapped in the building along with hostages under mortal threat.

As the slaughter begins, Morgan works alongside psychic Blake Daniel to discern the past of the staff, dating back to islands invaded by the Vikings generations ago.

Can Morgan and Blake uncover the truth before Ragnarok is unleashed, consuming all in its wake?

Day of the Vikings is a fast-paced, supernatural thriller set in London and the islands of Orkney, Lindisfarne and Iona. Set in the present day, it resonates with the history and myth of the Vikings.

If you love an action-packed thriller,
you can get Day of the Vikings for free now:

WWW.JFPENN.COM/FREE

Day of the Vikings features Dr. Morgan Sierra from the ARKANE thrillers, and Blake Daniel from the London Crime Thrillers, but it is also a stand-alone novella that can be read and enjoyed separately.

AUTHOR'S NOTE

As with all my books, the plot of *End of Days* is taken from my own experience and research of real places and events, twisted into an original story. For all the images behind the story, check out: www.pinterest.com/jfpenn/end-of-days

Why snakes?

I first handled a python in the Northern Territory of Australia when I was traveling back in 2000. The weight of its body, the smooth cool skin and the fact that I wasn't scared, all surprised me. Then I went into the desert of the Northern Territory and spent some time camping on the red earth, considered by the Aboriginal people to be the blood of the Waugyl, the creation serpent. I started to look into the mythology of snakes and found it fascinating. I actually bought a mulga wood snake at Uluru and I have it here beside me at my writing desk. I consider the snake to be my totem animal, so perhaps it was inevitable that I would eventually write a book with so many in.

I decided on the title, *End of Days*, before I had a plot idea. Then, when I read the verse in Revelation about the ancient serpent and discovered Lilith had been portrayed as a serpent in painting, I knew I could work them into a story that would also satisfy those longing for something apocalyptic.

Appalachian snake handling churches and venom as a hallucinogen

There are some fascinating videos on YouTube from churches that handle snakes, in accordance with the Great Commission of Mark 16:18. I wrote Lilith's scene based on reading about actual experiences of believers.

Some snake venom can be hallucinogenic, but it's likely to kill you first, so don't try this at home! Mithridatism is a real practice of self-administering venom in non-lethal amounts to build up tolerance over time.

Moses and the graven serpent

I have always found the story of Moses and the graven serpent strange. The snake is used as a symbol for evil in the Garden of Eden, and yet in Numbers 21:9, it becomes a bronze idol with healing powers and then in John 3:14, it's used as a metaphor for Jesus. These types of theological mysteries are where I often find story ideas.

When I visited Salisbury Cathedral and found the window above the altar, which is just as described in the story, I knew I had to use it somehow.

International locations

The Temple of Hatshepsut is real but as far as I know, there's no escape tunnel into the Valley of the Kings. Although if you look on Google Maps, it's definitely possible. The Laocoon is in the Vatican Museums and the replica stands in the castle at Rhodes. The Delphi site is as described.

Israel. I first visited Tel Megiddo in the 1990s and after reading James Michener's *The Source*, the area really came alive for me. I revisited in November 2016 and it was amazing to see the layers of history revealed at the dig. You can find all the pictures from that trip here: www.jfpenn.com/israel-pics

We also took some video of the trip, which you can view on YouTube:

- A Walk in the Old City of Jerusalem:
  www.jfpenn.com/old-city-jerusalem
- Behind the scenes of my research trip. Difference locations in Israel:
  www.jfpenn.com/israel-arkane-research

I did take some artistic license with the location. Most of the artifacts from the dig are at in the Rockefeller Museum, Jerusalem and other places away from Megiddo itself.

The Old City of Jerusalem continues to evoke my imagination and when we visited last, it was awesome to go down into one of the cisterns under the Holy Sepulchre, one of the few able to be accessed. The cistern used for the resurrection of the serpent may actually exist, although of course, let's hope that the sarcophagus is still deep in the Mariana Trench …

What's next for the ARKANE series?

While Morgan takes a well-earned rest, I'll be focusing on the United States of ARKANE. Jake heads to New Orleans to work with Naomi Locasto, who also featured in *One Day in New York*. In the last nine books, I've mostly focused on European history, so now I'm turning my gaze further west. Expect more ARKANE adventures to come!

MORE BOOKS BY J.F. PENN

Thanks for joining Morgan, Jake and the
ARKANE team. The adventures continue …

Stone of Fire #1
Crypt of Bone #2
Ark of Blood #3
One Day in Budapest #4
Day of the Vikings #5
Gates of Hell #6
One Day in New York #7
Destroyer of Worlds #8
End of Days #9
Valley of Dry Bones #10

If you like **crime thrillers with an edge of the supernatural**,
join Detective Jamie Brooke and museum researcher Blake
Daniel, in the London Crime Thriller trilogy:

Desecration #1
Delirium #2
Deviance #3

If you enjoy **dark fantasy,** check out:

Map of Shadows, Mapwalkers #1
Risen Gods
American Demon Hunters: Sacrifice

A Thousand Fiendish Angels:
Short stories based on Dante's Inferno

The Dark Queen

More books coming soon.

You can sign up to be notified of new releases, giveaways
and pre-release specials - plus, get a free book!

WWW.JFPENN.COM/FREE

ABOUT J.F.PENN

J.F.Penn is the Award-nominated, New York Times and USA Today bestselling author of the ARKANE supernatural thrillers, London Crime Thrillers, and the Mapwalker dark fantasy series, as well as other standalone stories.

Her books weave together ancient artifacts, relics of power, international locations and adventure with an edge of the supernatural. Joanna lives in Bath, England and enjoys a nice G&T.

* * *

You can sign up for a free thriller,
Day of the Vikings, and updates from behind the scenes,
research, and giveaways at:

WWW.JFPENN.COM/FREE

* * *

Connect at:
www.JFPenn.com
joanna@JFPenn.com
www.Facebook.com/JFPennAuthor
www.Instagram.com/JFPennAuthor
www.Twitter.com/JFPennWriter

* * *

For writers:

Joanna's site, www.TheCreativePenn.com, helps people write, publish and market their books through articles, audio, video and online courses.

She writes non-fiction for authors under Joanna Penn and has an award-nominated podcast for writers, The Creative Penn Podcast.

ACKNOWLEDGMENTS

Thanks to my editor, Jen Blood, for her help with the book, and my proofreader, Wendy Janes. Thanks to Jane Dixon-Smith for the cover and interior print design. Thanks as ever to my readers and to the Pennfriends, who encourage me to keep writing these stories.

CPSIA information can be obtained
at www.ICGtesting.com
Printed in the USA
BVHW030240240320
575821BV00001B/195